Valley
of Defiance

by Harriett H. Carr

WHERE THE TURNPIKE STARTS
AGAINST THE WIND
MIAMI TOWERS
WHEELS FOR CONQUEST
VALLEY OF DEFIANCE

Valley
of Defiance

HARRIETT H. CARR

THE MACMILLAN COMPANY · NEW YORK · 1957

Valley
of Defiance

Chapter 1

A brittle, creaking sound in the cold night wakened Walter Platt. For a moment he couldn't think what it was. Had he really heard anything? He pushed the quilts away from his ears and listened again, sure as his sleepy mind cleared that the sound would be repeated, and knowing what it was.

The bedroom floor planks groaned once more and Walter slipped from the warmth of the bed with its comforting soapstones and heavy coverlets. A pale December moon grayed the small, single-pane windows of the little room over the buttery which he shared with his younger brother John. In recent weeks Gerrit, the oldest of the three, had slept there too, leaving the front bedroom to his wife Lucretia so she could be more comfortable and near Ma. It was Gerrit who was up now and dressing. Walter could hear him fumbling with his clothes while he reached for his own heavy trousers.

"Go back to bed," Gerrit whispered. "You can't come."

Walter didn't answer. More words might waken John who was still sleeping soundly. It would be better if John knew nothing about this night's adventure. Not that Walter knew much himself, but John was only thirteen, two years younger than Walter, and not to be included in men's affairs yet. If he woke up he'd be sure to want to go with Gerrit too.

"I said you couldn't come!" Gerrit repeated.

Silently Walter buttoned his warm shirt, put on his coat and reached for his boots. Gerrit was tiptoeing toward the ladder now and as quietly as possible Walter followed. If they could get downstairs without being heard they would be safe. The ladder was next to the outside door in the buttery. No danger of knocking over any of the iron skillets or heavy crockery that Ma had stacked on the shelves that lined the four walls of the room.

Gerrit opened the latched door with a noise that seemed loud enough to rouse the neighborhood, and Walter closed it behind them more cautiously. Then they pulled on their boots, standing close to the walls of the "ell" waiting to see if they had been discovered. There was no sound from inside, nor any candle lit, and after a few minutes Gerrit started for the barn.

"You shouldn't come, Walt," he insisted. "This is no business for boys."

"Don't call me a boy," Walter answered. "You're only three years older."

Gerrit was bigger though. He had the shoulders of an ox, slim hips and strong legs. He was a handsome giant, this oldest of the three Platt boys, wiry like his mother and strong like his father, with waving light brown hair and blue eyes that usually were bright with laughter. There would be no laughter in them tonight though, Walter was sure.

Gerrit opened the barn door and the two stepped into the warmth of the stable. Ned, their shaggy mongrel dog, roused himself from his blanket on a bed of straw and came to them. Oxen and cattle munched their grain deliberately. There was a safe, reassuring smell of fresh straw and seasoned leather about the place and, standing close to the wall while he waited for his eyes to adjust to the blackness, Walter almost regretted his decision to go with Gerrit.

"How did you learn anything was afoot?" Gerrit asked, fumbling for one of the bridles that hung on a wooden peg in the wall.

"I saw you talking to old Sam Yates and the young fellows at singing school," Walter told him. "All of you shutting up like clams whenever John or I came near you. Of course I guessed something was up."

"You know Pa'll be mad if I let you come."

"He'll be just as mad if you go without me," Walter reminded his brother. "He's made it clear that he's against anything but legal action and it's no court of law you're riding to tonight."

"What we do is all the tenant farmers can do, and Pa should realize it," Gerrit said bitterly. "The laws are all for the patroons. Made by them and for them. They own New York state and run it for their profit."

Walter couldn't see Gerrit's face but he felt his own throat tighten and his thin jaw set in the darkness. Gerrit had reason to feel the injustice of the patroon system and Walter shared his brother's resentment. Gerrit and Lucretia had been married a year now, and soon they would have a baby, but Gerrit still had not been able to get a lease for any farm. There were few leases for sale and he couldn't pay the extra quarter of the lease price for those that were. The lease owner was supposed to pay it to the patroons but each one was trying to get the money from the buyers.

"Still, I don't feel right about letting you come along," Walter heard Gerrit saying. "You don't belong to the anti-rent association. I'm not sure they'd take you in yet, even though it isn't much of an organization."

"Maybe not, but I've got to know the arguments and decide where I stand, and before long, too," Walter insisted.

"You'll hear no discussions tonight!"

So it wasn't a secret meeting Gerrit was going to. It was something more serious than that. Walter tried to remember what he had heard of the uprisings in the Helderberg Hills after Stephen Van Rensselaer died in 1839. The anti-rent movement had started then, when the sons of the good patroon began ruthlessly collecting all the back rent old patroon Van Rensselaer had let slide. Pa had been opposed to those outbreaks of violence and kept reminding Gerrit that nothing good had come of it. Nothing had come of the peaceful, respectful petitions either, and this was 1843 with Gerrit desperate for a home of his own.

Walter's hands shook more with excitement than cold while he bridled his horse and led it out of the barn. He rode behind Gerrit in the shadow of the elms and weeping willows that lined the winding lane leading to the road. At the juncture Gerrit dismounted and in the faint light of a cloud-covered moon Walter watched him move stones from the sagging fence that outlined their father's fields.

"What are you doing?" Walter asked, his voice still low although there was no danger of any one hearing them now.

Gerrit removed a bundle from the pile of stones.

"It's my 'Indian' disguise," he explained. "No one should come out tonight without one and you haven't any. I can't let you come all the way."

"Where did you get it?"

Gerrit didn't answer. Walter watched him pull a shapeless calico dress over his coat and tie it about his waist with a wide sash of some plain material. The skirt came about to his knees and he had to pull it up to mount his horse. Then he covered

4

his head with a mask that appeared to be made of sheepskin, with four holes for eyes, nose and mouth.

"You don't look much like an Indian to me," Walter said.

"Perhaps not, but if we're seen no one can identify us," Gerrit explained, starting his horse off at a brisk pace. "You'll have to stay behind when we get to town because you'd be recognized. There's a safe place for you to hide though. That clump of pines back of the Dudley house across the road from the Ten Nuys manor."

Walter knew the house and the Dudley boys and girls too. They and Peter Ten Nuys all were tutored by Pastor Camp, and this winter Pa had been paying the minister to teach Walter too. Peter had resented Walter when he first came to town for schooling, and well Walter remembered their fight the first afternoon when lessons were over. Stouter by far, Peter had trounced Walter roundly. Then, satisfied with his victory he had impulsively offered Walter his own pocket knife, an act of generosity Walter would not have accepted if Pastor Camp hadn't insisted. The handsome Sheffield cutlery, a long silver bar in the haft, was safe in his pocket this minute.

Gerrit was hurrying his horse now and at the next cross-roads three other riders were waiting. Their incongruous head-gear and calico disguises were similar to Gerrit's, only these men had decorated their masks with squirrel tails or feathers.

"He's not going all the way," Gerrit explained quickly before any question was asked about Walter. "I couldn't make him stay home, but he understands he's got to hide in the trees at the edge of town."

The men hesitated and for a few minutes Walter feared he would not be able to go with Gerrit after all. Finally one man spoke.

"You stay behind, and git fer home fast when you hear

us starting back." The words were muttered in a deep, unnatural tone but there was no disguising the voice or the figure either. Sam Yates was almost as broad as he was tall. Anyone who knew him would not be fooled by that cotton wrapper. Looking at Gerrit, Walter was sure the mask and calico would be a poor defense if anyone saw him who knew those broad shoulders. Walter had a better build for the business—average height and weight with no peculiarity of walk or movement to make him distinguishable.

Walter tried to guess the identity of the others while he followed them toward town. Was Mr. Yates' nephew Tom among them? Tom Yates' father was dead and he and his mother lived with Sam and Mrs. Yates a mile distant from the Platt farm. Tom was Walter's age and his friend. Even in a disguise Walter would know Tom and he looked carefully for the square, squat figure but could not find it.

Gerrit was not armed in any way, but some of the riders they had joined carried axes and crowbars. They meant business and Walter wondered what they intended to do. If property was destroyed Pa certainly was going to be outraged, especially if he learned his own sons were in the raiding party. But why else would men carry such tools?

It began to snow before they reached the little crossroads town which was their destination. Gerrit held back until Walter had driven his horse into the cluster of trees at the back of the Dudley property, then rode forward with the others leaving Walter hidden in the blackness of the pines. For a time he sat astride his horse, straining his ears for a sound that would tell him what was happening. A dog barked in the distance, a night bird chirped woefully, and time was endless.

Walter slid off the horse's back and peered out of the trees toward the back of the houses ahead. There were no lights so he ventured nearer, keeping in the shadow of the trees that lined the road. Step by step, from tree to tree, Walter approached the front of the Dudley house. There was a light in the parlor, but who would be coming out at this hour, into a snowstorm? One more tree and he would be able to see the main street with its store and apothecary shop, the doctor's office and blacksmith shop, the tavern and next to it the patroon's land office.

The minute he thought of it Walter was sure the land office was the object of the night's raid. Emboldened by his curiosity he took a step or two into the street. Sounds of metal pounding against wood, of timbers breaking, became louder and more insistent. Then a dog barked again, loud and excited yelps. Another animal joined in, and the stillness of a few moments before was a noisy bedlam of barking dogs and crashing beams.

Walter heard a door open at the Dudley house behind him and he slipped back into the protection of the trunk of a big elm.

"What in tophet!"

It was Peter Ten Nuys' voice. Peter must have been visiting the Dudley girls and leaving at this late hour had discovered the "Indians" at their work. Walter could imagine the surprised look on Peter's round and florid face.

"Anna! Call you father!" Peter ordered. "Hurry! There's destruction going on."

Peter's heavy shoes pounded along the wooden walk that led from the Dudley house to the street, and Walter moved cautiously in the shadow of the tree to keep out of sight. Peter was not looking about the yard, however. Shouting loudly he raced toward the land office.

"Help! Men, get out here! Help!"

It was risky to stay longer but Walter had to see what was happening. Keeping the tree between himself and the

7

doorway he stepped again into the open street. At the far end a fire had been started, and to his horror he saw the disguised farmers tossing fagots through the battered door and onto the roof of the land office. No wonder Peter was calling for help. He could hear the shouts although a sudden swirl of snow hid his classmate's figure.

The land office was the headquarters from which Peter's father, Derick Ten Nuys, collected the rents from the tenant farmers in the township for the patroon. Old Derick Ten Nuys was like a patroon himself, livng in the largest house in town and presiding on rent day like a lord of the manor.

Recollection of Derick Ten Nuys brought Walter to a realization of his own danger. The big house across the street from the Dudleys' was the Ten Nuys home. If Derick had heard his son, and the "Indians" who had begun shouting war whoops of defiance, he would be out in another minute. So would Mr. Dudley. With a cautious glance in either direction Walter darted back to the precarious safety of the big elm trunk. The best thing he could do was get to the pines and his horse without being seen, but just as he was about to move back the Dudley front door opened. Out into the blustering night came Mr. Dudley, straight across his lawn toward the Ten Nuys house.

Walter had good reason to be thankful for the snow squall now. Circling the tree to keep out of sight he waited until he heard Mr. Dudley pounding on the Ten Nuys door and shouting to arouse his neighbor.

Darting from tree to tree, crouching under the shrubbery, his heart pounding as loud as his footsteps on the frozen earth, Walter made his way back to the pines and his waiting horse. There wasn't any need for him to hurry home ahead of the raiding party. Every man in the village would be rushing in the opposite direction to help put out the fire.

It wasn't long before pounding hooves told him the night's work was done. Walter waited at the edge of the road until he recognized Sam Yates and Gerrit. He fell in behind them without a word. They were riding silently and hard in the snow that had begun falling heavily.

At each crossroads men turned off to return to their homes, usually without a word. Only Sam Yates and two others who lived beyond the Platt farm were left when Gerrit and Walter reached their own lane. They waved to Gerrit when he dismounted to take off his disguise and return it to its hiding place in the old stone fence. Once again Walter looked for his friend but could not distinguish Tom among the masked riders. Probably Mr. Yates had not allowed him to come.

"You were right about Pa," Walter said when Gerrit remounted his horse. "I hate to think what he'll say when he hears what happened tonight."

"It wasn't as we planned it," Gerrit explained. "All we intended to do was break in and burn the rent records and those degrading work orders. I wouldn't have let you come if we'd planned to destroy property."

"You didn't intend to burn the land office?" It was a relief to know they hadn't actually plotted that destruction.

"No," Gerrit assured him. "That yelping dog and then Peter Ten Nuys upset us."

"Why did you start the fire?" Walter asked. "Didn't you have the records by the time Peter got there?"

"Yes, but we had to start the fire, don't you see?" Gerrit sounded annoyed. "It kept the men busy making sure the flames didn't spread, so we could get away safely. That Peter!" Gerrit went on. "He was the one who made the fire necessary."

Walter didn't answer. One could scarcely expect Peter

not to shout for help when the building his father was responsible for had been broken into and set afire. This was bad business destroying the patroon's land office.

"There'll be men riding after us now," Gerrit warned. "You can depend on it. The sheriff will have all of his constables and deputies out, snooping to find out who was guilty."

"The snow will hide our tracks, won't it?" Walter suggested. "How will they find out, once we get safe inside the house?"

"Look around the stables to see whether horses are blanketed and wet with lather from recent riding."

"We wouldn't dare not blanket the horses," Walter said quickly. "On a night like this, when they're overheated. We don't dare risk Pa's horses."

"Of course not," Gerrit agreed. "We don't dare risk getting caught, either. I'll stay in the stable and jerk the blankets off if I hear them coming. I can depend on Ned to bark, if I should fall asleep. Not that I'll sleep much the rest of this night. In an hour's time, though, there'll be no tracks and the animals will be . . ."

He didn't finish the sentence. At a bend in the winding lane they were suddenly in sight of the house. Except for their own low-ceilinged bedroom over the buttery there were lights in every window, upstairs and down.

Chapter 2

For an instant the Platt boys stared at their home while the horses took them nearer to it. Gerrit was the first to recover from his surprise.

"You take care of the animals," he directed and jumping from his horse ran across the yard and disappeared into the house.

A feeling of dread came over Walter. If anything had gone wrong with Lucretia while they were away, neither of them would ever forgive himself. Their disappearance had been discovered, of course, for whatever had roused the household, someone would have called Gerrit.

In the barnyard Walter found a one-seated carriage that did not belong to the Platts, and when he took the horses inside there was a strange nag in one of the empty stalls. Ned, roused from his bed again, rubbed against Walter's legs while he maneuvered the horses into their stalls and blanketed them.

Standing in the half-open door, watching the swirling snow, Walter began to wish he had not gone with Gerrit. He had been so eager to take his place with the men, to leave

11

John and boyhood chores behind. But what had happened while he and Gerrit were on this misadventure? Could the strange rig belong to Dr. Butler? And how long would it be before the sheriff reached the Platt farm? Gerrit could have guessed wrong about that. The officer might not come on such a stormy night, especially since it must be an hour or two past midnight by now.

Walter reached for the dog's head and scratched the flapping ears. He could depend on Ned to bark if any stranger turned into the lane, and he had to know what had happened. Shutting the dog inside the barn, Walter started for the house. He stumbled through the unlighted woodshed with its cords of firewood and axes stacked against the wall, into the buttery and thence to the kitchen. There lighted candles flickered on all four walls and over the dark brick fireplace where a black iron kettle hung above burning logs. No one was in the room and for a moment Walter stared at the familiar skeins of red and gray wool hanging over the spinning wheel, at the table and ladder-back chairs his grandfather had made, as though he had never seen them before. The room smelled of herbs—the herbs his mother boiled up in case of sickness. Bloodroot, dragonsfoot, balmwort . . . he couldn't identify the odors but from the bedroom above there came an unmistakable sound. A baby was crying lustily.

Walter let out a long sigh. So Gerrit and Lucretia had a baby with good, strong lungs. He smiled at the thought and wondered how soon he would be allowed to see it. Not until Ma told him he could go upstairs, of course.

A small hall and the steep stairs leading to the second floor bedrooms separated kitchen and parlor. Walter tiptoed across to peer into the front room. Candles were lighted on the walnut drop-leaf table and on a small desk. In their flickering light Pa sat reading the Albany paper. Under his homespun shirt heavy shoulders rose and fell with his deep breathing. His hair was as black as Walter's, his eyes as deep a blue, his full lips and firm face muscles gave him a young and vigorous appearance, although he was now a grandfather.

Pa didn't look up when Walter came into the parlor. The firm set of his chin confirmed Walter's fears. There was explaining to be done and his own jaws tightened as he prepared for it.

From his father's solid figure Walter glanced to the one picture in the room, where the waters of Niagara Falls seemed to move into the river. On the opposite wall a sampler, made by Walter's only sister before she died, called for God's blessing on the home. Remembering the playmate he had loved Walter wondered, hopefully, if Gerrit's baby might be a girl. Finally he walked into the room and sat down on the plain gray sofa which he had helped Ma repair last summer. With no daughter to help, Walter had been obliged to lend a hand at more than one household chore. They had stuffed the sofa with the tow of the flax which wasn't suitable for thread-making, and had covered it with the same gray lindsey woolsey Ma used for her men's shirts.

Walter traced the pattern Ma had stitched into the upholstery with a forefinger and waited. Pa knew he was there. Why didn't he speak up and get it over with? It seemed a long time before the paper was deliberately folded and set aside on the table.

"So you went night-riding somewhere tonight, and without permission!" Pa's voice was severe and accusing.

It was true. Walter said "Yes."

"A gathering of anti-renters?"

Walter nodded.

"I thought I'd made it clear where I stand on that matter." His father left his chair and walking to the fireplace kicked at a log with his heavy boot. "If Gerrit feels he must act for himself I suppose he's old enough and has that right. But you're not of age and I'm responsible for you."

Pa turned his back on the sputtering log and looked down at Walter. "You understand that, don't you?"

"Yes, but I've got to make up my own mind about these things," Walter insisted. "I'm going on sixteen and I can't help thinking for myself, even if I wanted to."

"Thinking indeed! I hope you're really thinking. From the record of the anti-renters, that's something they don't do. If people would think before they act, there'd be fewer mistakes made."

Walter knew what his father meant. Gerrit had married before he had a home to take his wife to, so he'd brought Lucretia here to Ma and Pa. Now he had a family and still no home. Pa had never favored Lucretia, either. She was so slight and fairy-like, with light yellow curls and pale blue eyes, and she depended on Gerrit for every thought and act. It was hard to imagine Lucretia ever doing the work Ma did from sunup to sundown and then spinning by candle light. Not that Lucretia hadn't tried to do her part of the work.

"This isn't the time to talk about it," his father went on. "Ma's got to get something for the doctor to eat and she'll need a hand. It was a mercy I knew Mrs. Bell had been worse and that I might find him there, what with you two off with both horses. But tomorrow I want to hear all the arguments and we'll see whether you've done any thinking or not. Gerrit . . ."

Pa didn't have a chance to finish the sentence. From the barn came the sound of Ned barking wildly.

Walter jumped to his feet, "Pa, it's the sheriff! I left the horses blanketed and that's a dead giveaway."

He started for the kitchen, but his father's strong hand

14

on his shoulder swung him around. The blue eyes were dark with fury now.

"The sheriff! Then there was mischief afoot tonight!"

Walter pulled away. "Let me go! I've got to get to the barn ahead of him."

But Pa held him firmly by the shoulder. "Were you disguised? A disguise is more damaging than blankets on the horses."

"I wasn't. They'll never find Gerrit's."

"Is it here? About the house or barn? It mustn't be found here! There's a law against wearing disguises."

"It's not here! Let me go, Pa!"

Walter pulled away from the relaxing fingers and dashed into the kitchen. He was at the woodshed door when he thought of the tracks he would leave in the snow. There was another way to get to the barn though, and into it too. Grabbing a knife from a box on the shelf beside the fireplace, Walter let himself out of the kitchen window, closing it quickly behind him. With the knife he could lift the lock on the one window in the back of the barn and get inside.

The barn was only a few paces from the house, and the lane leading from the main road was long and dark and winding. In less than a minute Walter was pulling the blankets from the horses, even taking time to fold them as they should be. The animals were no longer damp with sweat, and that was a relief to him while he clambered back through the barn window and raced for the house. He was safe in the kitchen, pulling off his snow-covered boots, when he heard a knock at the front door.

The parlor floor boards groaned when Pa crossed the room. Walter gritted his teeth and waited. Pa couldn't turn his own son over to the sheriff, no matter what he'd done. But never in his life had Pa been known to tell a lie. What would he do now?

A blast of cold air swept through the parlor and into the kitchen when Pa opened the door and held it wide. Heavy boots were stomping on the steps outside.

"Why Sheriff! What brings you out at this hour?"

The surprise in Pa's voice sounded so genuine that Walter could almost believe it.

"Come in. Never mind the snow," Pa boomed.

"It's a sorry business I've come on. I want to see Gerrit Platt."

"Gerrit?" Again Pa sounded surprised. "Come in, don't stand there in the storm. Gerrit's made me a proud man to-night. He's presented me with a grandson!"

"What?"

"He's upstairs with Dr. Butler. I'll go get him. Maybe the grandson too."

Out of sight, Walter slumped onto the three-legged stool beside the fireplace. He should have known Pa'd not let Gerrit down. Pa's footsteps were heavy on the uncarpeted stairs as he hurried up and soon the boots of Gerrit and Dr. Butler were clambering down behind him. Walter couldn't see them but he could hear Gerrit whispering "There-there" when the baby started crying again.

"What's up, Sheriff?" Dr. Butler asked as soon as the three were in the parlor. "I hope you aren't asking the father of a first-born son to ride out with you on any posse work tonight."

"Well, that ain't what I come fer," the officer admitted and he sounded uncomfortable. "The fact is, I was told Gerrit was with a bunch of anti-renters who burnt the patroon's land office tonight."

"What?" Pa and Dr. Butler gasped in surprise.

"Peter Ten Nuys said he could recognize Gerrit's broad

shoulders even with a disguise, no matter how hard it snowed," the man went on, and Walter squirmed on his stool at the words. "It was Peter who discovered the 'Indians' at their dirty work."

"Well, I don't know anything about what Peter Ten Nuys said, nor what happened in town tonight, either," Pa said firmly. "You see what you see, with your own eyes and in this lighted room, not in the black of night and in a snow storm. And you know where I stand on disorders and rioting. I made that clear when the outbreaks first began. I haven't changed."

"I know, I know," the man agreed. "But Peter Ten Nuys . . . I guess I'd better take a look around . . . in the stable."

"You might find the horses still damp," Dr. Butler spoke up. "Mine too. We didn't waste any time nor favor the horses in getting here."

So Dr. Butler was protecting Gerrit too, although he well knew Gerrit hadn't been there until a scant hour ago. Out of sight in the kitchen, Walter tried to recall what he knew of the physician and how he looked. Thin and stoop-shouldered, dark hair and eyes and a beard that usually looked as though it needed trimming, he remembered.

"We're about to get the doctor something to eat," Walter heard his father saying. "A cup of tea would warm you up too. You're welcome to it."

"No, no, thankee jest the same. I'll look around and be on my way."

"Don't mind the dog," Gerrit said, speaking for the first time. "I'll go with you if you're afraid, but he won't bite."

"No, no." The sheriff hestitated. "Congratulations on the boy." Then the door banged behind him and the parlor was very quiet.

"I hope Walter's at least got the water hot," Pa said but

now his tone had changed and become sterner. He had protected Gerrit but he had not condoned nor forgiven his sons.

Walter jumped to his feet and peered into the kettle Ma had left over the fire. It was half full and near boiling. He'd make the tea, but now he must see the baby. He hurried to Gerrit's side as soon as the three men came into the kitchen.

Neither the danger he had been in nor Pa's indignation could lessen Gerrit's pleasure in his son. He smiled happily and moved the warm blankets away from the little face so Walter could glimpse his nephew.

"He's a Platt, Walt," Dr. Butler announced. "Looks just like you and your father and young John. Gerrit's the only one who favors his mother."

Pa didn't look at either Walter or Gerrit. He went into the buttery, closing the door behind him. From there he could watch the sheriff without being seen. Gerrit took the baby back upstairs and the doctor, with a weary sigh, sat down beside the bare kitchen table.

There seemed to be nothing for Walter to say while he took dishes from the corner cupboard. Ma had baked dried apple pies the day before and fresh bread. There was smoked meat in the buttery and he'd get that as soon as Pa came out.

Pa returned almost as soon as Gerrit was back downstairs.

"Well?" Dr. Butler asked. He looked very thin and tired and he pushed his scraggly hair back from a high forehead with a nervous gesture.

"He's gone," Pa said. "Didn't even look in the barn. Maybe he was afraid of Ned."

"Now that it's over, tell us what happened, Gerrit," Dr. Butler said, motioning to a chair.

Walter avoided looking at his brother or Pa who was towering over him.

"All we intended was to burn the rent records, and those

work orders, so Ten Nuys couldn't stand there on rent day like the patroon himself, directing us to give our service and we agreeing like so many serfs," Gerrit began.

"And then?" Dr. Butler prodded.

"Some dogs set up an infernal racket and Peter came out and discovered us. Then we tossed the lighted papers onto the land office roof and into the doorway, so everyone in town would have to stay there and put out the fire. I don't believe the place could have burned completely. The snow would help control the flames."

"Under the circumstances, I guess that was the smartest thing you could have done," Dr. Butler said and stretched his legs out into the room.

"The smartest thing they could have done!" Pa thundered the words. "What were they doing in the first place? Breaking in and destroying records! No law-abiding citizen . . ."

But Dr. Butler interrupted. "Sit down, Platt. My father helped toss tea into Boston harbor once. He was a General in the Colonial army. Maybe he wasn't a law-abiding citizen either, but he fought to free this country from tyranny. Now, a generation later, how free are you? And your sons? And this fine new grandson?"

"I'm not saying the patroon system is right," Pa argued but he didn't sit down. He stood in his dimly lit, smoke-stained kitchen head and shoulders above everyone except Gerrit who had gotten to his feet and was standing behind his chair, fists tight over the back slats.

"My father could only give me a lease and that's all I can pass on to one of my sons," Pa admitted. "This house that I built and the orchard I planted all belong to the Van Rensselaers. But those are the legal terms of the lease and burning and rioting won't change them."

"Perhaps that's where you're wrong," Dr. Butler contradicted. "Over in Rennselaer County my fellow physician, Dr. Smith Boughton, is the leader of the farmers who are up in arms. He's the 'Big Thunder' you must have heard about. He's urging open defiance in support of petitions. It's the only way to show the legislature that the farmers mean business."

Pa shook his head but didn't answer and the doctor went on.

"Everywhere in the Hudson River Valley the farmers are in revolt. They've got to make themselves heard or this thing will go on forever."

"I'm glad to hear you say that." Gerrit turned away from Pa. "We in the back clearings can't go on paying tribute forever, never owning the land we cultivate. We pay taxes while the patroons pay none. They make the laws and we obey. I've got a son now and I want to own the land I work, and be able to pass it on to him, free and clear."

It was the first time Walter had ever heard Gerrit stand up to Pa, and Pa was quick to answer him.

"Then work for it openly and honestly like a man, not hidden in a false 'Indian' disguise." Pa was shouting now, his face flushed and hard in the flickering candlelight.

Gerrit rubbed his clenched hands against his hips. "Pa, for four years the farmers have been signing petitions. I say it's done no good."

"You're wrong there, Gerrit," the doctor interrupted calmly. "Petitions do good. The more names on petitions, the surer indication that the farmers are organizing. But Dr. Boughton says it will take petitions backed up by open demonstrations."

"And I say no son of mine can ride with the raiders and burn and destroy, and live under this roof!" Pa declared his position, looking from Dr. Butler to Gerrit. "There were men killed in the Helderberg region and there'll be more lives lost if this keeps up. Do you understand me, Gerrit?"

Furtively Walter looked at his brother. Gerrit's handsome features were heavy with anger, his fists still clenched at his sides. He looked at his father without a trace of contrition.

"You give me no choice for now. I understand."

Unexpectedly Pa wheeled and faced Walter.

"And you! You're going on sixteen. You think you're a man who must make up his own mind. That's all right. But I say you cannot ride with the 'Indians' and live here as my son. Is that clear?"

For Walter, too, there was only one answer even though he was sure Dr. Butler and Gerrit, and the leader 'Big Thunder' whose name was echoing up and down the valley, were right. He choked on the words but he said them.

"Yes, Pa."

Then he turned to the boiling kettle over the fire. Would he and Gerrit be able to keep out of this revolt for justice now flaring openly in their own township, after tonight?

Chapter 3

Walter spent the next day whittling spiles from sumac branches so there would be a supply ready when sap began to flow from the maple trees in another month or two. In each eight inch length he carved a trough for about six inches, leaving a round plug at one end that could be tapped into the tree trunks. Through this solid end of the branch he forced a hole. Thus the sap could trickle down the trough and into the waiting sap buckets.

It was tedious, working alone at the job. John was with Pa at the sugarhouse checking on sap buckets and gathering pails. Gerrit had ridden off alone, without explanation, as he had done more than once lately. So Walter was at the house with Ma and Lucretia and the job of making new spiles to replace those lost or damaged after last spring's sugaring off.

Lucretia was spinning, one slender foot on the treadle the other rocking the plain wooden cradle where baby Elias kicked and cooed. Her curls were bright as the winter sunlight that streamed through the kitchen window. Once or twice when Ma was out of the room she glanced at Walter questioningly, as though she wanted to say something, but he immediately busied himself with his whittling. If she wanted to ask where Gerrit was, he didn't know the answer. Or if she knew and wanted to tell him, he didn't want to hear. Gerrit should tell them where he went on these unexplained absences. The whole family was tense and touchy, for no one knew where he was going or what he was doing unless it was Lucretia.

It was late afternoon now and Lucretia kept watching the lane, anxious lines between her eyes. Even Ma seemed worried, although she bustled about the kitchen to buttery talking about the food she was preparing and avoiding any mention of Gerrit.

"Clean up your mess now, Walt," Ma directed, stopping long enough to survey the afternoon's accomplishment. "Spiles are the one thing sumac's really good for, I guess. The berries do only a moderate job of coloring."

Ma's hair was a soft gray but her eyes were still bright hazel and she had no more wrinkles than Lucretia. A calico apron covered her dark red-brown woolsey dress, dyed with the sumac berries she belittled .

"Lucretia, you'd best set the table for supper. I heard Pa and John banging milk pails a minute ago. They'll be here soon, and starving."

Ma's ears and her timing were right. The salt pork was fried to a golden brown, the dried corn simmered in rich milk when John and Pa came in.

"What do we get for supper?" John asked at once, sniffing the savory odors. "I could eat a bear. Raw."

John was a slender boy, thinner than Walter and his eyes, under long black lashes, took in everything in the room with a quick glance.

"Easy for you," he scoffed at Walter. "Whittling spiles in a warm kitchen while Pa and I . . ."

"When you learn to do carving you can have the job," Walter interrupted. "You have to be careful with the knife, whittling spiles. It's not altogether to my liking."

"What is?" Pa asked, looking up from the wash basin where he soaped the flakes of sugarbush bark and dirt from his face. "That's something you should be thinking about."

Walter had no chance to answer. Not that he knew what he would say. There were so many jobs around the farm he didn't like, and he had probably complained too often. But now feet were stamping on the woodshed steps and through the buttery. Gerrit opened the kitchen door, motioning Sam Yates in ahead of him.

"Why, Sam! Good evening," Pa greeted him. "You're just in time for supper."

"Sure I ain't intruding?" He pulled off his knitted gray mittens and coat, needing no urging. Ma motioned Lucretia to set another plate and told Walter to put a log on the fire in the front parlor.

Sam Yates was past middle age. His hair was straight and almost white, his light blue eyes watered. When he crossed the room Walter was certain Mr. Yates was the "Indian" leader who had allowed him to accompany Gerrit on the night of the raid and he wondered what had brought him home with Gerrit tonight.

The talk was of the weather and the prospect for an early sap run at the table, but as soon as they had finished Ma's berry pie the men started for the parlor, Walter and John following.

"John, you haven't brought in enough wood," Ma called, banishing the youngest Platt from the discussions Walter knew were about to start among the men.

"Oh, Ma!" John protested while his reluctant feet started for the woodshed. "Why can't Walt do it tonight?"

Ma shook her head firmly. Walter was pleased she had not found a chore for him too; that she was letting him take his place with the men.

Gerrit didn't sit down when Pa motioned toward the parlor chairs.

"It's time I told you where I've been lately and what's afoot," he began, standing near the fireplace, his fingers combing his short hair. "I asked Mr. Yates to come with me tonight and confirm it. The farmers in this township have agreed not to pay rent this year on Rent Day. We've talked it over and that's the decision. We wish it was unanimous."

Walter stared at Gerrit in disbelief, but Pa heard the news as though he had expected it.

"Sit down, Gerrit. Don't stand there like a preacher." Then, turning to Mr. Yates, "You aren't going to town Friday with your rent?"

Mr. Yates sat with his hands gripping his knees and he shook his head slowly. "I'm not going, Platt. Nobody's going unless it's you."

So that was to be the farmers' next move. Mr. Yates and Gerrit had been organizing them and without letting Pa know, so he couldn't present arguments against the plan.

"We know how you feel about rioting and most everyone agrees with you, Pa," Gerrit went on. "But we've got to do something to show the patroons we're fully behind our petitions. We've got to force a change in the feudal leases."

"There's only two ways we can act, Platt, as I see it," Mr. Yates substantiated Gerrit. "Rioting and disturbances, or acting in unison and refusing to pay rent until we get justice."

Pa didn't answer at once. "Your wheat was pretty skimpy last harvest, I admit," he said finally. "Everybody didn't get good crops." He was staring at the fire, forming his words deliberately.

25

"That ain't the point, Platt," Mr. Yates insisted. "You've got good land and three sons to help you. My land's wore out and buckwheat's the only crop I can depend on. My only son left these parts as soon as the Erie Canal opened a route to cheap land in Michigan. All the help I have is my nephew, Tom."

He drew a long breath, but went on before Pa could speak again.

"You've built yourself a good frame house and we still live in the cabin my grandfather built of peeled elm logs, roofed with poles. But that ain't the point. It's been two generations since the Revolution made us a free country, but here in the Hudson River valley we ain't free. We've got to do something, Platt!"

He leaned forward, his fat sides bulging against the arms of the chair, perspiration gleaming on his forehead.

"If we all stay away from the land office on Rent Day, the patroon will have to take note, Pa," Gerrit insisted. "That's what all the men in this township have agreed to do. Elsewhere too."

"Who's been stirring them up to that decision? You?" Pa asked.

Gerrit didn't deny it.

"You and the young hotheads in the neighborhood, I'll wager," Pa charged.

"Them and their fathers who own nothing but leases and can't pass the land on to their sons," Mr. Yates said. "We're the ones to decide how best to do something for ourselves and our children."

Walter felt his cheeks burn at Sam Yates' words. The man made it sound as though Pa was taking sides against his own sons. The spitting logs in the fireplace were the only sound in the uncomfortable stillness of the little parlor until Pa finally spoke.

26

"This spring the legislature meets again, Yates," Pa began. "You signed the petitions with the rest, asking relief from distress. Those petitions should be presented and acted upon before we do anything more."

Sam Yates shook his gray head and pounded his knee with his clenched fist.

"Dr. Butler told me there would be 25,000 names this time," Pa went on. "Horace Greeley's *Tribune* says the legislature can't disregard that many people."

"Horace Greeley down in New York! Oh Pa!" Gerrit scoffed.

Pa didn't answer Gerrit or move from his chair and Gerrit made one last appeal.

"Won't you stay away from the land office on Rent Day?" he asked.

"No, because I think this move is wrong," Pa said deliberately. "I don't want to risk losing what I've got. You must realize . . ."

But Gerrit interrupted. "Then you'll go alone!" He shot the words out, his shoulders squared in angry opposition to Pa's decision. "I'll not go and hand over the grain we raised to Derick Ten Nuys and take his work orders like a slave!"

Sam Yates got up and lumbered toward the kitchen where he had left his coat.

"Maybe you'll change your mind, Platt," he said speaking more calmly than Gerrit. "I'll be leaving now. I've said all I can say."

Gerrit went with him and did not return to the parlor. The clock on the mantle ticked loudly and Gerrit's steps resounded on the stairs when he went to join Lucretia and the baby in the room above.

"Well, Walt, I guess you've heard most of the arguments," Pa said at last. "I've a good piece of land I can pass on, either to you or John, whichever seems most likely to be a good farmer and wants it. I'm worried though. I'm not a lawyer but as I see it, the farmers are breaking their leases if they refuse to pay rent. If the patroon has nothing but trouble, and no rent coming in, what's to keep him from taking the leases away?"

That was an argument Walter had not heard before. Perhaps Pa had intended to present it when Gerrit interrupted him. Now that Walter thought about it, the possibility was frightening.

Pa got up and shoveled ashes around the smouldering logs in the fireplace. He placed a heavy hand on Walter's shoulder before starting upstairs.

"Try to think reasonably, Walt," he said. "I leave it to you whether you take Gerrit's place and go with me on Rent Day."

It was a long time before Walter closed his eyes that night. John had taken hot soapstones to their chilly bedroom over the buttery and already was fast asleep when Walter crawled into the warm bed. He had wanted the right to make up his own mind and Pa was giving it to him, but whose judgment was best, Gerrit's or Pa's?

Suddenly something Pa had said came back, as clearly as though Pa were there in the room repeating his words:

"I've got a good piece of land I can pass on, either to you or John, whichever seems most likely to be a good farmer and wants it."

Walter stiffened at the memory. He had known Pa could not divide the land . . . that he could pass the lease only to one of his sons. Gerrit had faced that reality and was bending every effort to get another farm and make his own way. Pa was still a vigorous man who would work the land for many years. John was the one who should get the lease, so what was Walter to do in the future which now seemed suddenly upon him? He recalled Pa's question at supper time too. What was to Walter's liking? He turned restlessly, remembering everything that had been said while he waited for sleep to come.

At breakfast the next morning neither Pa nor Gerrit mentioned the previous night. Gerrit was a cheerful as though there had been no argument and no ultimatum.

"I'll go to the sugarhouse if you'd like, Pa," he offered. "You haven't finished checking on the buckets and gathering barrels have you? Maybe John would like to help me."

A grin immediately lightened John's face and he pushed his plate away. He as well as Walter had always been eager to participate in any activity with Gerrit, and Gerrit hadn't mentioned Walter this time. With a good-natured nod of triumph John went for his coat and cap, and soon he and Gerrit were singing as they started for the sugarbush.

Gerrit as well as Pa was allowing Walter to make up his mind himself.

Walter looked at the pile of sumac branches he had arranged neatly in the corner of the kitchen the night before. Pa had started for the barn and the day's work. The grain had to be measured out, poured into bags and loaded on the wagon to be delivered as rent tomorrow. Four fat hens must be caught and penned in a carrying crate. Pa could do it without help but he never had done it alone. Gerrit always helped and rode to town with Pa. Together they had accepted their work orders.

Walter knew his mother watched him while he hesitated in the warmth of the kitchen. Lucretia waited too, and he couldn't look at her nor at the laughing boy in the cradle. Gerrit and little Elias must have a fair chance in life and so must he and John, but now Walter knew what his decision must be. He took his coat from its peg and left the kitchen.

In the shed next to the barn Pa was counting grain bags. Walter took the peck measure to the wheat bin and waited. When Pa came he handed Walter a bag and for a moment he stopped and smiled.

"A man only has to make one decision at a time, Walt," he said. "I try to do what seems right each step, as it comes along. I'm glad you decided to stay by me this time. Now you hold the bags and I'll fill and count."

Walter felt good while he watched the shining kernels slide from the wooden measure into the bags. Pa was cool and level-headed. After they'd finished counting he'd ask what Pa thought he should do to make his way in the world, but first he'd say that John was the one who ought to have the lease.

Walter had no chance to talk to his father that day, however. At mid-morning a shadow in the open shed door drew their attention. It was Tom Yates, rifle in hand.

"You're busy, ain't you?" Tom greeted them. "I was going hunting and I thought Walt might come along. Ma packed fresh bread and butter and maple sugar cookies and apples." He patted his bulging pockets.

"The woods are full of rabbits," Pa said, straightening up. He and Walt both knew Sam Yates had put down precious little pork or beef for the winter. The Yates family depended on wild game for the table.

"I'll tell you what," Pa proposed. "You catch the four hens for us and tie their feet together, then Walt can go."

Tom propped his rifle against the side of the shed and took off his coat. Soon the barnyard was a tumult, with hens squacking, Ned barking, and feathers flying. Pa and Walt both laughed at the sight of Tom's squat figure puffing behind the Plymouth Rocks, stumbling when his straight brown hair blew into his eyes.

"Run along and help him," Pa said. "We're almost

finished with the grain. I can manage. Maybe you can bring a rabbit or two home for us."

The merriment was over as soon as the hens were caught. Then Walter and Tom were on their way to the woods, each thinking his own thoughts.

"Are you going with your Pa tomorrow?" Tom asked, stretching his short legs to keep up with Walter's longer strides.

Walt slowed down. "How did you know what Pa's going to do?"

"That's been all the talk at our house for weeks," Tom said. "Who's going and who ain't. I know you went with Gerrit, too. Uncle Sam wouldn't let me, though I wanted to. Who do you suppose made Gerrit's disguise?"

"I don't know. He wouldn't tell me."

"It was Maw!" Tom sounded proud. "Walt, what's there going to be for you and me if the anti-renters don't win?" he demanded seriously.

Walter had scarcely thought of his own problem until a few hours before. Confronted with Tom's situation, he had no answer.

"A lease can't be passed on to a nephew," Tom went on. "All I can do is follow young Sam to Michigan, I guess. Land's for sale there cheap, only I've got no money at all, and Maw doesn't want me to go any more'n Lucretia wanted Gerrit to go."

"What?" Walter demanded. "How do you know so much?"

"Talk's free at our place," Tom said knowingly. "With Uncle Sam heart and soul in the movement, and getting information from 'Big Thunder', the men bring their cider jugs to our place and tell him everything."

"Did Gerrit say he wanted to go to Michigan?" Walter

demanded. Gerrit had never mentioned such a move at home.

"He said there was no use talking. He couldn't tear Lucretia away from her folks. I can just see her crying and carrying on at the thought, can't you?"

Walter closed his lips firmly. Tom probably was right. Gerrit took Lucretia home to see her mother and sister almost every Sunday but Walter hadn't thought much about it. Gerrit always took the horses and carriage, while the rest of the family crowded into the ox cart to go to church, but no one had spoken a word of criticism. Walter wasn't going to say anything against Lucretia now, and he and Tom crossed the back field to the woods in silence. Tom sat down stockily on the first fallen log, rifle beside him.

"Let's eat," he suggested. "This is as good a place to watch as any."

Walter sat down near him and Tom spread the food between them. Over their bread-and-butter lunch their eyes met, and Walter saw his own anxiety in his friend's face.

"What is there for a farm boy who ain't got a farm?" Tom demanded. "I don't blame you for going with your Pa tomorrow. I'd go with Uncle Sam if he was going. But what about you and me, Walt?"

Walter shook his head. "I don't know, Tom. I'm getting more worried all the time."

Chapter 4

January first had been Rent Day as long as Walter could remember. In years past he had ridden on the back of Pa's sleigh as far as the main road, chickens squacking in their crate beside him, wheat in the loosely filled grain bags slithering beneath his hands and knees, and Ned barking a cheerful send off. He recalled the noisy greetings that had echoed along the clearing when Pa and Gerrit joined the train of wagons and ox carts all heading for town. Today Pa's oxen followed an empty, snow-filled road. Above them a red-headed woodpecker beat angrily at a resistant tree trunk; the doleful cawing of a crow sounded in the woods ahead. Even the hens they must forfeit in tribute to the patroon were silent at the back of the load.

Walter sat beside his father on the one seat at the front of the sleigh, blankets wrapped snuggly about his knees, and tried to think how he would bring up the subject he wanted to discuss, now that he and Pa were alone. He couldn't remember ever having talked seriously with Pa about anything personal before. Not that he hadn't taken problems to his father—how to fix the harness the time it snapped, how to rescue the puppy from an abandoned well after John had playfully tossed the dog in. Pa had always known what to do and he would have something to suggest now, Walter felt sure.

"Pa, I've been thinking," Walter began, but unexpectedly his father raised a hand for silence. He was leaning forward on the seat, head turned sidewise, eyes alert. Walter listened. Above the steady clomp of the oxen and creaking of the runners there was a strange, skirring sound he could not identify. He turned to his father wanting to question him but afraid to speak.

Pa let the oxen go forward slowly. His face was stern, his eyes narrowing. The rhythmic hum continued, growing louder when they came to a bend in the road. Walter saw his father's head come up with a jerk and followed his eyes to the tree tops on either side of the road. One huge oak in a cluster of trees was swaying heavily, the last brittle leaves falling loose in the motionless morning air.

"Oh!" Walter exclaimed, suddenly cold with fear. He knew that sound now. Someone was felling the giant oak. Where would it land when it came down? Were they far enough away to be out of danger?

Pa jerked the oxen to a halt and stood up in the sleigh, one hand out as though to ward off a blow, his face grim while he watched the swaying tree, his body tensed and ready to leap. With the screech of a wounded animal the trunk groaned and crashed to earth ahead of them, its force sending up a swirling spray of snow. There it lay, an unmovable road-block, barring their progress.

Pa let out his breath slowly, watching the road and listening. Even the crows were quiet and there was no human sight or sound. Handing the reins to Walter, Pa got out of the sleigh and walked slowly into the clump of trees. He was a big man and Walter had no fear for him. If the men who had cut that tree to keep him from going to town were waiting, there would be a fight. No voices came from the brush however, and after a few minutes Pa returned, carrying a heavy stick in one hand and walking fast.

"They didn't dare face me," he told Walter and began unhitching the oxen. He handed the branch to Walter when he had finished.

"Start banking the snow against the trunk on either side, while I go home for a shovel and planks," Pa directed. "It would take us all day to move that tree, if we could with just the two oxen. We've got to drive over it. And we've got to be prepared for more roadblocks ahead."

Walter watched while his father turned the oxen toward home. He wondered if the men who had felled the tree were waiting in the woods, watching. If they were they offered no resistance when Walter began building a ramp of snow, pounding it down with his heavy boots.

Who had done this, he wondered while he worked. Had Gerrit known an attempt would be made to prevent Pa from paying the rent? Gerrit hadn't been away from home since the night he had brought Sam Yates with him to talk to Pa.

What about Tom? If Tom had known, he could not have kept it to himself, Walter was sure. But some of the neighbors were so opposed to Pa that they had almost stopped him. Walter felt his cheeks burn at the thought. No one was willing to bow to the patroon this year but his father.

It wasn't long before Pa returned. He was steadying the planks across the oxen's shoulders and he had brought shovel, chains and ropes. Within an hour they had built a ramp on either side of the tree and skillfully Pa maneuvered the animals and sleigh up one side and down the other. Then he and Walter gathered up their equipment.

35

"There's no knowing what we'll encounter before we get to town," Pa said when he started the oxen again. "Keep your eyes open."

They watched and listened every step of the road but there was no further interference. When they came to the clump of trees back of the Dudley house Walter pointed to them.

"That's where I hid while the others rode into town that night," he confided. "Gerrit wouldn't let me come farther."

"I'm glad to hear it," Pa said. "I'm glad Gerrit didn't let you ride into danger. There's plenty of it afoot in this region now, I'm afraid."

It was the first time Walter had been in town since the night the "Indians" had set fire to the land office. He half expected to see Peter when they drove past the Ten Nuys' big house. It stood aloof on a sloping hill like a castle, with the back of the house on a lower level than the entrance. Stretching from the road to the rear door were the rose gardens which Mrs. Ten Nuys opened to townspeople on Sunday afternoons in the summer. They were a gaunt network of thorny bushes, dark against the snow today, and there was no life about the place.

There was little life in town, for that matter. Two empty wagons were hitched in front of the tavern but they had not come from Walter's neighborhood and he had no way of knowing whether they had come laden with produce for the patroon.

"In other years the yard has been full, and we've waited all day for our names to be called," Pa told Walter. "Horses whinnying and stomping, men cold and anxious for the cheer of the inn."

Walter was surveying the land office rather than listening to Pa. A blackened place around the door and repairs to the roof testified to the fire, but otherwise the weather-beaten wooden building that looked so like a prison, was no different. He was glad the fire had not done major damage.

Pa drove close to the one large, open window where the men turned in their grain and at once Walter saw the stocky man inside. Derick Ten Nuys must have been handsome in his youth. His round face was bearded along the chin now, and his big hat was pulled down over his forehead, but his features were even and his chin strong. He didn't wear homespun, even for the work of taking in the rent. Peering through the window into the bright sunshine he recognized Pa and called out the name.

"Elias Platt."

It wasn't a greeting, it was a roll call. At the name Peter appeared. He looked like his father, though he had no beard. His young face flushed and his jaws hardened when he came to the window.

"Hello, Peter," Walter said, feeling self-conscious and uncomfortable. Peter looked at the load and didn't answer. From the paper in his hand he called for the rent due, his voice high-pitched and unnatural.

"Forty bushels of wheat!"

Pa and Walter jumped from the sleigh. With his greater strength Pa lifted the bags from the wagon box and Walter helped him pass them through the window. They could hear Derick Ten Nuys telling someone where to place them, but only father and son were in sight, receiving and counting the rent. Walter wondered how they knew what was due, since the "Indians" had destroyed their records. Probably from years of collecting, they remembered. In any event, Pa was not given any accounting and had nothing to say about the amount demanded.

When all finally had been passed from the wagon into the

land office, Pa stood straight in the cold outside. Walter stood beside him, not knowing what would happen next.

"Elias Platt," Mr. Ten Nuys read again as though once more calling roll and not looking at Pa. "Four days' service on the roads."

Pa repeated, "four days" and turned to the sleigh. The transaction apparently was over. The Ten Nuys, who attended the same church with them—Peter, who had shared Walter's lessons and his play—had not recognized them as people. Hadn't spoken to them except to announce the rent and service due.

Walter had not known it would be like this. No wonder Gerrit and the other farmers were indignant. He felt resentment and humiliation too. Had Pa accepted this high-handed treatment for so many years that it no longer affected him?

Cheeks burning, Walter walked around the sleigh to get in beside his father, but just then Peter came out of the building. He looked about the empty yard and across the street to the tavern, then came directly to the sleigh.

"Where's Gerrit?" he demanded of Walter. "Why did you come today instead of Gerrit?"

"Gerrit's working in the sugarbush," Walter started to explain, but Pa interrupted.

"Gerrit expects to get his own lease this spring," he said. "He won't be coming with me any more. Walt took his place today."

"I might have known he wouldn't show his face!" Peter spat the words out, still addressing himself to Walter. "I was waiting for him and he knew it. He didn't dare come himself, did he?"

"Of course he dared!" Walter shot back. "This isn't his business any more."

"Didn't the sheriff give you a satisfactory report on

Gerrit?" Pa asked more calmly. "He came to our place saying it was you who directed him."

"The sheriff is a rummy old fool!" Peter scoffed. "All you had to do was give him a swig of that stuff you back clearing farmers brew . . ."

The tone and the charge were too much for Walter. No apples from the Platt orchard ever went for hard cider. He swung straight for Peter's chin and the blow caught him unprepared. The other boy reeled backward against the land office building.

Pa jumped from the sleigh and caught Walter by the shoulder, holding him firmly.

"Get into the sleigh, and no more of this!" he ordered his son.

Peter started toward them but Pa put his big weight between the boys, his back to Peter and the land office, and Walter obeyed with alacrity. What if Derick Ten Nuys had heard the angry voices and came out?

"Go home!" Peter was shouting as Pa started the oxen. "Go and tell Gerrit I'll settle with him yet!"

Walter didn't speak while Pa drove to the tavern. He had been wrong and he would take his punishment, whatever Pa felt was due. To his surprise Pa didn't speak until he had tied the animals.

"You go to Pastor Camp's and tell him you're coming for lessons again, regularly," Pa said. "It's time you were back in school and we'll find the money. It costs little more than the bill from the common school. Stay for this afternoon's classes. I'll get the tea and raisins and stuff your Ma wanted at the store and wait for you here."

Relieved, Walter left the tavern yard.

Only the cemetery separated the parsonage from the white-spired church where almost everyone in the village and countryside came to worship. The church was chilly and badly heated in winter, but Pastor Camp's parlor would be warm with glowing logs and filled with boys and girls busy at their lessons. Walter straightened his hat and brushed away the flakes of straw and seeds that had clung to his suit before knocking at the door. Remembering the "Indian" raid and Peter's bitter charge, he wondered how he would be accepted. If Peter had been talking against Gerrit everywhere, perhaps he wouldn't be welcomed here either.

The minister came to the door in response to Walter's knock.

"Walter Platt! This is a surprise," he said but he didn't sound surprised. He was a slender, stoop-shouldered man of middle age, with thin brown hair parted in the center and brushed straight back from a high forehead. His blue eyes were troubled and the half-opened door seemed a rejection of Walter. For a moment Walter hesitated, wishing he could go away; wishing he could get out of town entirely without seeing any more people. But Pa had said he was to go back to school.

"Pa said I could come for lessons regularly," Walter began. "He said to tell you we'd pay the fee . . ."

Pastor Camp was shaking his head. He coughed and wiped his lips with a wrinkled handkerchief.

"I can't take any more to tutor, Walter," he said looking away from his own doorstep toward the snow-drifted street and the land office beyond. "I've been sick since Christmas." He coughed again. "I can't take any more."

From the moment Pastor Camp opened the door Walter had known something was wrong, yet the words came as a shock. Pastor Camp, the dominie to whom he had turned for direction all his life, was sending him away. How could such a thing happen?

"I hope you'll be in church Sunday?" It was a question, asked a little more forthrightly.

"I don't know. I guess so."

"And Walter, I hope you'll go on with your studies." The minister dropped his voice almost to a whisper. "Go to the common school, even if you don't like it. You're a good student. You'd make a real scholar."

Walter shook his head and turned away. The teacher at the common school didn't know as much about arithmetic and little more of reading than Pa, and he kept order by threats and beating on the desk with his ruler.

"I'm sorry," he heard Pastor Camp saying. "I mean it, Walter, and I do want you to go on to school. You're one of the brightest."

The door was closing. Embarrassed at his rejection and sick at heart, Walter said good-bye and turned away. Uncertain what to do, he started for the store. Pa would be getting the things Ma wanted and he might stay quite awhile visiting. It would be cold waiting in the sleigh in front of the tavern.

The store was on the same side of the street as the land office and Walter wanted to avoid that place. He had an uneasy feeling that Peter had been watching. Perhaps Derick Ten Nuys had told the rector not to tutor the tenant farmers' children any more. Never before had Pastor Camp shown any distinction between town boys and those few, like Walter, who came from the farms. Walter walked slowly and didn't look up or cross the street until he was opposite the store. Peter, however, had no intention of letting him escape as though unnoticed.

"You 'Indians' will find out how civilized people feel," he shouted. "Dare to attack the patroon's property again and you'll find out!"

Walter gritted his teeth and hurried up the three or four

steps to the ice-crusted porch of the store. Pushing the door open, he stepped quickly into the dim warmth inside. Long counters stretched the length of either side of the room and in the back was the section behind a cage where people came for their mail.

Pa was in front of the cluttered grocery counter. Cheeses and moulds of maple sugar that farmers exchanged for tea and flour and staples were piled in front of him. At the opposite counter a large, plainly dressed woman was unrolling bolts of flowered dress goods while she waited her turn for attention. The shelves that lined the wall were loaded with sewing equipment and rolls of cloth, all intended for the ladies' fancy.

A frigid blast that came in with Walter brought all eyes to the door. One surprised look and Pa seemed to understand what had happened. His lips tightened and he assembled his purchases hurriedly. The storekeeper's curiosity had to be answered though.

"Did Pastor Camp turn you away?" the thin old man asked. "Your Pa jest told me he was puttin' you back fer tutorin' and I wondered when he said it."

"Wondered what?" Walter asked, resentful that his private injury was being exposed here in the store, and hoping he could keep his feelings out of his voice.

"I jest wondered how far the patroon has had Derick Ten Nuys go," the merchant answered and he sounded sympathetic. "Old Derick had Pastor Camp give Peter a letter so the boy can read law with the dominie's relations. Pastor Camp wanted to pass that plum out himself to the best in the class. He told me so himself. But Peter's got the letter and I guess a law office only takes one beginner at a time."

He peered at Walter through small, metal-rimmed glasses and pushed at the merchandise in front of him in an anxious way. Across the room the woman had stopped her examination of the dark wool material to stare and listen. The merchant seemed almost to be talking for her benefit although he ignored her presence completely.

Walter wished he had not come to the store. Before he could think what to answer, even more humiliation was heaped upon the Platts.

"If I wuz you I'd be an 'Indian' instead of payin' rent," the storekeeper said to Pa. "If Pastor Camp has to turn farm boys away, you know why. Is there anythin' else you want?"

"No!" Pa's answer was quick and curt. He took his packages, handing some to Walter to carry, and they left the store at once.

Until they were out of town Pa did not speak. In the cold silence Walter felt his father's anxiety and dismay. That morning his neighbors had given him grim evidence of their disapproval. In town no one had welcomed them, not even Derick Ten Nuys who took their grain and hens. Worst of all was to have their pastor turn Walter away. It wasn't likely Pa would feel like going to church again after this last blow, and neither would Walter.

When Pa spoke it wasn't to mention Pastor Camp or Walter's future schooling. His information was unexpected.

"The storekeeper needs a boy, Walt," he said. "The poor old fellow fell on the ice, first storm we had, and broke both shoulder bones. He can't lift and haul any more."

"What? You don't mean . . . ?"

"He hinted he would take you. Before you came in. I told him I wanted you to get schooling but it's precious little more you'll get at the common school."

The long, bony rumps of the oxen swayed in unison before Walter's eyes and the bare roadside brush moved slowly past while he thought about it. Here was a way out; a way to avoid taking sides in the struggle that was shaping up between patroons and tenants. But Walter wasn't looking for a way out. Peter's face, surly with anger and disdain, Derick Ten Nuys turning away from Pa without recognition, were as plain before his eyes as the jogging oxen.

"What I want is a way to help end the patroon system forever," Walter said. "I've seen it first hand now and I've had enough. I've got to take my place in the fight, Pa."

Pa ignored his declaration. "Think about the storekeeper's offer," he advised. "It's a good chance, and you're the one who's got to be next to leave the old farm."

Somehow it didn't surprise Walt to learn that Pa had come to the same conclusion as he had reached. He was the one to follow Gerrit. But not, he resolved, until the battle for freedom had been once more fought and won.

Chapter 5

Before they had turned from the main road Walter knew something was wrong at home. First there were men's voices, some angry, some taunting, mingled with Ned's excited yelps. Rounding the bend in the lane, both Pa and Walter exclaimed aloud in surprise. Half a dozen masked men, all on horseback, were milling about the barnyard. Standing in front of the barn door, shotgun in hand, was Gerrit, flanked on one side by John and the other by Tom Yates.

There was no quickening the oxen but when the first masked rider saw them, all turned from Gerrit to await Pa. Their stomping, whinnying horses and their bright-colored disguises were a strange sight in the somber Platt barnyard.

Pa drew the animals to a halt and stood up in the sleigh to face the "Indians." "What's the meaning of this?" he demanded.

"Perhaps you've not heard that the farmers in this region are standing together, Platt!" Walter couldn't recognize either the voice or figure of the man who seemed to be the leader. "We're cutting off the manes and tails of all horses belonging to them that don't stand with us. Everywhere you go, you'll be a marked man. Everyone'll know you stood for the patroon instead of your own kind and kin. Mebee you'd of been for the British in the Revolution, too!"

"Pa, listen to me!" Gerrit called. "You promised me animals and tools to start farming, as soon as I get a lease. I've earned it, you always said. Give me the horses and they won't be touched. Everyone knows where I stand."

Gerrit was gripping the old gun in both hands and standing in front of two determined looking boys as though he were protecting them too. Inside the barn the horses were snorting in response to the excited animals outside. In his mind Walter, could see the flashing tails and waving dark manes they still might loose.

Pa didn't answer at once and Walter was beginning to fear he would refuse when he finally faced the spokesman for the "Indians."

"Will Gerrit's proposal satisfy you?" he asked. "It's true I expect to set him up as soon as he gets a lease. You can see for yourselves that he didn't go with me today to fulfill my obligation."

Hoots and jeers greeted Pa's words.

"Obligation!"

"Help the patroon instead of your own sons!"

"Traitor!"

Pa ignored the abuse.

"If the horses are Gerrit's, will you be satisfied?" Pa asked again. "If you're from these parts and know me, you know I keep my word."

The angered riders gathered to one side and Pa and Walter left the sleigh to go to Gerrit. Deliberately Pa stepped in front of John.

"Don't shoot, whatever they do," Pa said quietly to

Gerrit. "Put the gun down if there's fighting to be done. We'll try to protect the horses."

Walter counted the men again while he waited for their decision. There were six, and with John and Tom Yates Pa had only five to defend his animals. But there was no fight. The leader alone rode up to them, the others starting for the lane.

"We'll not touch your horses this time, Platt," he said. "You're a man of your word and Gerrit's one of us. But understand this. Everywhere in New York state except the Hudson River valley, the farmers own their land. We're going to own ours, and them that's not for us are against us!" He kicked his horse in the ribs and followed his companions out of the yard.

Gerrit set the gun against the barn and wiped his perspiring forehead. John was the first to start talking.

"If it hadn't been for Tom they'd have got the horses," he began breathlessly. "He came rushing to the sugarbush to warn us."

"We couldn't let it happen," Tom said shaking his head until the scraggly hair fell down from beneath his old hat. "They came to Uncle Sam wanting his Unit to join them. Nobody along this road wanted to."

"I didn't think it was any of the men from around here," Gerrit said and he sounded relieved. "I looked at all the horses and couldn't recognize them, so it must have been members from nearer town."

Pa lay a kindly hand on Tom's shoulder. "I'm glad it wasn't the neighbors and I thank you for warning Gerrit. I hope your Uncle Sam knows you did this, and that it's all right with him."

"I didn't ask him, but he knew what I was up to when I left," Tom assured him.

"If you'd asked, he might have thought he had to say no," John suggested. "It was just as well you didn't ask."

Walter thought that was very probable. Sam Yates would have been torn by the question. He was thinking also that when Gerrit finally left home, there would be no member of the anti-rent movement in the Platt family to stand with the united farmers and protect their home and property. When Tom started for the lane, Walter walked with him.

"Tom, how old do you have to be to join your Uncle's group?" he asked as soon as they were out of hearing.

"Eighteen I guess, but I don't know."

"I've got to join!" Walter said it deliberately. "Can you find out how?"

"Maybe. I want to join too," Tom told him. "If they let you, they'll have to let me."

"Then find out. There must be things we can do to help before we're eighteen."

Tom promised and kept his word. After the sugaring off was over and before planting time kept all men on the land, a new Unit was to be formed. The meeting was to be held deep in Sam Yates' woods at his little sugarhouse.

Walter didn't tell Gerrit of his intention to join. In his own mind he was convinced that the Platt family had to be associated with the movement officially or the neighbors might have nothing to do with them. How did Pa think he could have a husking bee in the fall if no one would come, and who would come if Gerrit was gone? There hadn't been a singing school at the Platt home since the night when the "Indian" raid was being planned. Each time the young people met someone had quickly offered to be the next host and the Platts had accepted and said nothing.

Once more Walter waited until John was asleep before slipping out of bed and creeping silently down the ladder and out of the house. The moon was full and he made good time crossing the open fields, but once in the heavily-treed Yates woods he had to go more slowly, feeling with his feet for the faint trail worn by the runners of the sled during sugaring off. Less light filtered through the umbrella of branches overhead, now full with bursting buds or the first filigree of leaves. Once he stopped at the sound of footfalls behind him. It could be a panther or a bear and he was not armed. Few had been seen in the country recently, he reassured himself. More likely an elk or moose deer.

Walter wheeled and clapped his hands together. Immediately branches crackled and a huge shadow, eighteen or nineteen hands high, dashed away with rapidity and no regard for the racket that echoed in the midnight stillness of the woods. Walter could see no antlers, but the male lost its horns each spring and this animal was too large to be anything but a male moose.

"For an 'Indian' you're making a tremendous racket!"

The words startled Walter but the chuckle that followed reassured him. Dimly he made out the figure of Sam Yates, garbed in calico and with the sheepskin mask over his face.

"Am I late?" Walter asked. "I was slowed in the woods where I couldn't see very well."

"You're the last. There'll be fifteen in your Unit and your Chief is the only one except myself who knows the identity of all. You'll know him only as 'Yellow Jacket.' If you do learn who he is, you're not to tell. You aren't supposed to know me, for that matter."

Sam said it seriously, in a low voice, while he led Walter to a circle of men beside the sugarhouse. There he took charge.

"It must be known that two in this new Unit aren't eighteen years of age and don't have horses of their own. They

49

might not be able to come, if summoned, but they can be of service."

He paused, then went on ponderously, as though he had memorized his speech and was reciting it by rote.

"These youngest valiants are to be equipped with tin horns which they will sound if the sheriff or any of his deputies are seen on the road. If the officers come, it will be to evict some tenant farmer or to sell his stock, for rent not paid last January. We must expect that, and be alert to sound the alarm with these horns. Then we can assemble from all directions before the sheriff descends on his victim. By peaceful means we can protect our rights, through the superiority of our numbers."

Mr. Yates breathed deeply when he finished, then moved from man to man distributing horns to those who had not provided their own. When he came to Walter he handed him a package also.

"This disguise was made for you to avoid embarrassment at home," he said. "Hide it where no one can find it, but keep your horn where you can get it in a hurry. If anything happens you should lose it, ring the dinner bell to warn the neighbors on the farm beyond you. They'll take up the alarm. The sheriff won't come to your place, but the rest of us . . ." He left the sentence and its chilling implications unfinished, and for a few moments the men in the new Unit neither shuffled their feet nor coughed. Then a husky voice spoke; a voice Walter did not know.

"Are you ready to take the oath?"

The recruits chorused, "We're ready."

One by one they repeated it, after their leader. Walter felt his throat tighten and his voice was unnatural when it came his turn.

"I do of my own free will and accord come forward to join this body of men, promising in the presence of

Almighty God that I will do all in my power to support the constitution; that I will go at all times when deemed necessary; and will reveal no secrets of the Society made known to me, necessary to be kept, and stand by each other as long as life lasts."

There was a strained silence after the last man had taken the oath, then Yellow Jacket addressed his Unit.

"You may not have heard, but the judiciary committee of the legislature has issued a savage report. It denounces Governor Seward and all members of the legislature for inciting the farmers to action. They're angered too by the great number of names on the petitions presented a few weeks ago. The landowners have formed what they call a 'Freeholders' Committee of Safety' and they've had 1,000 copies of the report printed by the *Catskill Recorder*. I have one or two copies if anyone here knows of a person who should be informed how the farmers are being denounced."

The full implication of Yellow Jacket's words came to Walter instantly. This leader did know his identity, and without mentioning his name, was speaking directly to him. Pa was the one who should see that report and know the result of peaceful petitions. Already Walter had an assignment.

"I'll take a copy if there's one to be had," he spoke up, wondering how he could get it into Pa's hands without explaining where it had come from. Then, unexpectedly, from across the circle of men who had pledged to stand by each other as long as life lasts, came another message for Walter.

"There's an old man in Schoharie County, name of Abe Harrison, who has a lease for sale. The rent's higher than in Rensselaerwyck. Tenants loose their farms after the death of the second person named in the lease, so this Harrison is anxious to sell and save something. He can't pass the lease on. He's the second named. Besides, he has no son."

To give this information to Gerrit meant revealing what

he had done, but Walter was sure Gerrit would not condemn him. Gerrit could openly give the judiciary report to Pa, too. With a feeling of relief he put the paper safely inside his coat pocket and started home. He'd hide his disguise in the old stone fence with Gerrit's, and keep the tin horn on a ledge along the sloping outside entrance to the root vegetable cellar under the house.

Walter had an opportunity to talk to Gerrit alone the very next morning. Ma kept her bags of dried fruit, her honey and cakes of maple sugar in the loft and after breakfast she sent John scrambling up for supplies. In the same breath she said she needed a ham and sausages from the smokehouse and Pa offered to get the meat for her. Gerrit and Walter started for the barn together.

"I've a message for you, Gerrit," Walter confided as soon as the door closed behind them. "Abe Harrison in Schoharie County has his lease for sale."

With a start Gerrit faced him, lines clouding his smooth forehead, his eyes half-shut and serious.

"What have you done, Walt?"

"The Platts have to be represented in this movement," Walter defended himself. "You'll go, and what will happen to us then?"

"You'll go next, and soon enough. Haven't you thought of that? Pa's got to make a different decision."

"Maybe this'll help him." Walter took the report from his pocket and handed it to Gerrit, explaining what it was so Gerrit would not take time to read it now.

"You can give it to him openly," Walter suggested. "I'd rather he didn't know what I've done."

"I should say not!"

Gerrit sounded severe but the next moment he put his arm around Walter's shoulders.

52

"So you'd protect Pa and the family. And Lucretia and me. But you've got to start thinking of yourself soon, Walt. You must realize that."

"I do." Walter nodded, remembering. "The storekeeper in town wants a boy and it's a good chance, but somehow when I think of weighing tea the rest of my life I want to give up! Look, Gerrit, can I go with you when you see Mr. Harrison?"

"If Pa'll let you. I'll ask."

Pa let Walter go. They started at daybreak the next morning and rode as fast as the horses could go until near noon when they came to the Harrison place. There was a small log house with a frame ell that probably had been added years ago when Abe Harrison brought his bride home to live with his people. At one side of the house there was an apple orchard and beyond it a planting of plum trees. Three rectangular fields stretched to the woods beyond.

"Walt, while I'm talking terms with Mr. Harrison, you look over the place," Gerrit suggested. "Pa's taught you how to tell good land, same as me."

They knocked and Mrs. Harrison answered. She looked to be about sixty-five, bent and with teeth missing on one side of her mouth.

"We heard the lease was for sale," Gerrit explained. "Is that right?"

"Come in, come in! Pa's up and around today, but he's a little deaf and you'll have to speak up."

"Can my brother look about the place while I talk to him?" Gerrit asked.

Mrs. Harrison said "Sure thing" and Walter left, glad that he didn't have to shout at Mr. Harrison.

"Be sure to look at the sugarbush," Mrs. Harrison called after him. "We're right proud of that."

53

The orchard was in good shape with apple trees pruned and clear gravel around the plum trees to keep the earth moist and let water through. Walking along the rail fence with its interlaced white pine poles, Walter found a good growth of gooseberry and currant bushes. White pine was a good tree and best for shingles and building timber. At the edge of the woods he took stock. More white pine, hickory which was excellent for fuel and for farming tools, basswood, butternut and sugar maple, all trees found only in soil that would be good for grain, too. There were even a few black walnut, a tree never found except in strong and durable ground.

Walter followed the trail into the sugarbush. Mrs. Harrison hadn't misrepresented it. Fencing had kept animals out and there were about fifty trees to an acre. Young saplings had been thinned too, and cut for wood. The bush had a heavy crown development to protect it from the sun, and walking over the bed of humus, which had been kept free of grass and weeds, Walter estimated the bush to be two or three times the size of Pa's, or maybe more. This was a good farm. The rough log sugarhouse was in firm shape. Peering through the windows he could see rows of sap buckets, huge boiling kettles, and stacks of pound molds.

Walter took his time, sizing up everything. He had a good report for Gerrit when he reached the house but he found his brother coat in hand, and ready to take his leave. Mrs. Harrison walked with Gerrit into the yard.

"You see how it is with us," she was saying soberly. Then, to Walter, "You found everything as I said?"

"Everything. It's a good farm." Walter felt enthusiastic, but looking from Mrs. Harrison to Gerrit he knew some obstacle stood in the way of the sale. Gerrit was shaking his head.

"I don't see how I can do it," he said. "I'll have to see

whether there is any way I can raise the quarter sale money. Good-bye."

"What's wrong?" Walter asked as soon as they were out of the yard.

"The owner claims a quarter of the sale price and if Mr. Harrison turns it over, what's left is too little for them to live on," Gerrit explained. "They want me to pay a quarter over and above the price of the lease and I can't ask Pa for it. I don't think he has it, and besides it isn't fair or right!"

Walter had very little idea of how much money his father might have saved during the years he had worked the Van Rensselaer land. Pa had a good farm and he was frugal, but there had been the expense of his sister's long sickness and finally her death. Other expenses came to Walter's mind. A new wagon last year, an ox to replace one that had died when bit by a rattlesnake before Pa discovered it. He might have saved the beast with a poultice of pounded waterpepper if he'd known sooner.

"The owner's going to check what the next tenant has in the way of stock and farming tools, too," Gerrit went on. "They won't approve a lease from anyone who hasn't a superior plow and a drag and harvest tools for grain and hay. It all adds up to $150 or more. I'd figured I could exchange work for tools with some of the neighbors, the first year. Unless I sell all my own cows but one, and Pa can get a loan for me, I can't meet those terms."

It was a blow, especially since the Harrison farm was good. Silently they jogged along the miles that separated them from home, Walter thinking how ideal the place was for Gerrit and Lucretia, for it was an equal distance from her home farm and his.

Walter forgot his disappointment when he rode into town. He had dreaded this part of the trip in the morning, but he and Gerrit had not seen either Peter or his father then. It was too much to expect they could ride past both the land office and the Ten Nuys' home twice in one day without meeting one or the other.

Walter looked apprehensively ahead at people in the street. In front of the land office several men were gathered, all intent upon appraising a lean cow. It was Gerrit who recognized them.

"Walt, look! The sheriff's taking someone's cow in to Ten Nuys, I guess."

"They must have forced a sale in spite of the 'Indians,' " Walter agreed. "Let's try to ride past without stopping."

"Just ride slowly," Gerrit advised. "They may not pay any attention to us."

The men were in an animated discussion when Walter and Gerrit rode alongside, Peter's outraged voice shouting above the rest.

"Five dollars! Are you telling me that's all you got?" He looked up then, and surprise replaced the anger on his face.

"Well! Gerrit Platt! Where have you been? Riding with the savages again?"

Gerrit slowed his horse. "I've been about my own business. Is that enough?"

"Not quite," Peter answered and his insolent tone aroused Walter's fury again as it had at their last encounter. "Sheriff, were these fellows in the crowd that accosted you today?"

The sheriff stepped away from the cow to peer at Gerrit and Walter. "I'd say they weren't," he answered nervously. "Didn't they just ride up from the opposite direction?"

"They could have circled around," Peter insisted. "Where have you been?"

"Look here, Peter, I don't like your insinuations," Gerrit answered, keeping his voice steady. "It's none of anyone's business, but I've been investigating a lease. One that may take me out of Rensselaerwyck."

"And a good thing. We've had enough of your tin horns and calico."

Gerrit slid from his horse and faced his tormentor.

"I don't know what happened here today for I've been over in Schoharie County, but if you have anything more to say to me, or accuse me of, let's have it."

Walter held his breath. In spite of Gerrit's seeming calm, resentment burned in his cheeks and tensed the muscles of his neck. Peter was no match for Gerrit, and Walter feared the sheriff might be called upon to take action that could go hard with his brother if there was a fight. Peter, however, had no intention of engaging in a battle he could not win.

"I have something more important to take care of now," he answered, gesturing toward the sheriff and the cow. "You may not have been with your 'Indian' horde today, but don't forget I know of the night when you were!"

He turned sharply, dismissing both Gerrit and Walter. Gerrit remounted and with a quick slap at the animal's shoulder and a nod telling Walter to follow, led the way out of town. They were well past the Ten Nuys manor before Gerrit spoke.

"Walt, did you think you recognized that cow?"

"No, I scarcely looked at it."

"If I'm not mistaken that lean animal with its bony hips was Sam Yates' cow," Gerrit told him. "Come on, let's get home."

Pa was waiting at the main road when they reached home, his hand shielding his eyes against the red rays of the setting sun. Trailing beside him was one of the Platt cows, at the end of a heavy rope.

"What happened?" Gerrit and Walter asked at once.

57

"The sheriff came to take Sam Yates' animals for rent due," Pa explained. "The alarm didn't get through to him and the neighbors beyond because of you two!"

"What?" Gerrit and Walter both exclaimed.

"That's what!" Pa sounded angry. "You could have told me you were to spread the alarm with tin whistles or by ringing the dinner bell. I heard the racket at the Tanner place but I didn't know it was a signal. So the sheriff got through."

Pa's words silenced both Gerrit and Walter. Because of them Sam Yates had lost one of his cows and he had only two. That wasn't all though, and Pa told the story indignantly.

"The first thing I knew the Tanner boys were riding past, all feathers and calico. They shouted that the sheriff was just behind, and where were Sam's cattle and oxen? They rode right on to his place without stopping. I figured the oxen would be at the back edge of the woods, so I got a whip and called Ned, and between us we lashed the beasts into the woods where they couldn't be found. In the meantime the sheriff was at the house and when I got there he said he was holding a sale, then and there. Said he'd posted notice, but where nobody knows. The old patroon would never have allowed such a thing!"

"The old patroon's gone, Pa. There's no more leniency in cases of distress," Gerrit reminded his father.

"There was none today," Pa agreed. "The sheriff had brought along a man to buy, and he got the cow for a pittance, because none in the crowd would bid. Then the 'Indians' tried to form a circle around the other cow and stop the sale. I guess the sheriff lost his head. He shot to drive them off and killed the cow."

"Killed the cow!" Walter repeated the sickening words.

"So you're to take this heifer over right now," Pa directed. "They can't get along without milk. I don't know how you boys feel about this, but I think we should give the cow to Sam, not just loan it."

Walter and Gerrit looked at the sleek animal Pa had brought. It was one of the young heifers Gerrit had considered his own—one he probably had been thinking he could sell. He hesitated when Pa pressed the rope on him.

"I thought you were the one who pledged to stand by, Gerrit!" Pa shot the words at him. "Maybe you, too, Walter for all I know. However that may be, we're not seeing Sam Yates go without necessities. He's bad enough off as it is."

The oath he had taken in the presence of Sam and Tom Yates came back to Walter at Pa's words. It was Pa who was living up to the spirit of it. Walter edged his horse between Pa and Gerrit.

"Come with us, Pa," he urged. "You did more today to help Sam Yates than anyone. We'll all go together. How can any of us keep out of this?"

Chapter 6

Disconsolate and defeated, Sam Yates sat on the top step of the entrance to his home, Tom at his feet. In the yard half a dozen of the neighbors sprawled on the grass, some still wearing calico wrappers, their discarded masks strewn in disarray beside them. All were watching the Platts while they made their slow way along the path, Pa on foot and trailing the cow behind. Animosity or incredulity were plain in the faces that stared up at Walter in the early evening sunset.

"Sam, we've come as neighbors," Pa began. "I guess Gerrit has something to say."

Gerrit slid from his horse. "If I'd been at home the alarm would have gone through," he began. "Or if Walt had been home. We both knew the signal, but we neglected to say anything to Pa. Now all we can do is give you this heifer, but with a young cow you'll be all right."

Sam's heavy shoulders straightened and he wiped his face with the back of a grimy hand. In the awkward silence a robin chirped its bell-clear night call; grazing horses snorted as they munched the new grass.

"I wasn't blaming you, Platt," Mr. Yates said at last, looking from Gerrit to Pa who still was holding the rope. For a moment Walter wondered if the offer was going to be rejected. Were the Platts to be repudiated by all of their neighbors? Then Tom spoke.

"If it hadn't been for Mr. Platt we might have lost the oxen too," he said, pushing his unkempt hair back from his forehead. "It was him and his dog that drove 'em into the woods and kept 'em out of sight."

The men shifted positions and looked at one another uneasily. When one of the Tanners spoke, Walter was sure he recognized the voice of "Yellow Jacket" and he listened intently, keeping his gaze on the rope in his father's hand and trying not to change expression.

"Somebody saved the oxen," Mr. Tanner said slowly. "We didn't have time. Was it you, Platt?"

"Sam Yates has been my neighbor and my friend all my life," Pa answered. "There was no justice in trying to impoverish him so he never could get a start again. I don't think the sheriff's sale was legal, with no notice posted in these parts. There should be justice within the law."

"You've seen with your own eyes how much we get from the new patroon," Sam said. He pulled himself to his feet heavily and walking the two or three steps that separated him from Pa, took the extended rope. "I wish I didn't have to take your cow, but you know I'd do as much . . ."

He stopped in the middle of his sentence. The sound of rattling buggy wheels and pounding hooves brought the men in the yard to their feet. Sheepskin masks and calico disguises were rolled into bundles which Mr. Tanner quickly gathered together. Looking about the yard for a hiding place, he spotted the low-hanging branches of a scrub pine in the yard which Tom was pointing out.

61

"Give me a boost. I'll tie them up high and out of sight with one of the sashes." Tom said.

Feigning unconcern, the men seated themselves on the grass again, waiting for the new arrival. As soon as the rig was in the yard there was general relief. Dr. Butler handed his reins over to Tom with a nod of greeting. Walter left his horse to take the cow's rope from Mr. Yates and lead the animal to a grass plot.

"I got here as soon as I heard," Dr. Butler began, seating himself on the top step. "I should have been in this neighborhood before, but there's been so much sickness this spring." His voice trailed off in a weary sigh and he began filling his pipe slowly.

"Is it true that the sheriff killed your other cow, Sam?" he asked between puffs. "That's the story in town."

Sam nodded. "We'll have fresh beef for a spell, which is more'n we've had all winter. The missus is fixing coals for roasting some of it now, so stay and eat with us. All of you. She's baking fresh corn bread too."

"We may as well make a party of it," the doctor agreed. "That's more than is happening in town. When Ten Nuys found out the sheriff only got five dollars and both your cows were gone—well, young Peter was talking of having the man removed."

"I'm not surprised," Walter spoke up, remembering the scene in town. "Peter seemed more bitter than his father when Gerrit and I saw him this afternoon."

"He's more or less taking over," Dr. Butler told them. "Making a lot of trips to Albany for his father. Trying to work into a job of some sort with the patroon, I presume. But that's not what I came for."

His voice suddenly commanded attention. Dr. Butler had not just happened to drop by.

62

"Agents are being sent out from Rensselaer County to organize everywhere, from Orange to Albany counties." He got to his feet and addressed himself to the little group of men with unexpected forcefulness.

"The resistance movement has got to be stronger than petitions and 'Indians' trying to prevent seizures, like today's. It's developing into a strong political action, with men delegated to get candidates into the legislature who'll pledge in advance to change the laws. Big Thunder is asking all tenant farmers to assess themselves two cents an acre to build up a fund. Then you'll elect representatives to act for you, and campaign to see the right men run for office and get elected. There are eight or ten of you here. Enough to do the work in this township. What do you say?"

"I'd favor that," Pa spoke up immediately. "I'll make my contribution as soon as I can get to town and sell some maple sugar, but there's one thing I'd like to see made part of the record."

"What's that?" Dr. Butler asked.

"This should be an outright, open action and apart from all rioting and raiding done by mobs in disguise."

"That's the new plan," Dr. Butler advised him. "There's nothing in it to keep members of the old 'Indian' Units from belonging, though."

Pa looked thoughtful and Walter feared he might offer objections, but Dr. Butler had anticipated his reaction.

"If the old 'Indians' weren't allowed to participate, there wouldn't be enough men left to make any kind of an organization," he said. "Now what we propose is to take our cause to the legislature and the courts. There are lawyers who claim the old Van Rensselaer title and some of the other landlords' titles aren't valid. The first Van Rensselaer got his grant from the Dutch. It was confirmed by a charter granted by the English governor in 1685 and by the English crown in 1704. The first state government recognized it when New York colony became a state, but still, it's for the courts to decide. And there's certainly a question as to the legality of the terms of the leases, and of the quarter sales that are demanded every time a lease is sold."

"There is?" Gerrit asked eagerly. "That's all standing between me and a good lease right now. I can't raise that quarter sale."

Less chance than ever, now that he had to part with his heifer, Walter was thinking.

"Don't pay it," Dr. Butler advised, turning his attention to Gerrit. "Help collect assessment money here in your township and wait until Big Thunder sends word of the next move, and who to elect to the assembly. This may be a long fight, but it's headed in the right way now."

The men began planning immediately, all talking at once. Walter stood at the edge of the group feeling left out, and when Pa noticed him it was not to bring him into the planning.

"Walt, hurry home and see if Ma hasn't some pies or maple sugar cookies she can send over, or maybe a kettle of beans. There are a lot of people here for Mrs. Yates to feed."

Walter couldn't refuse, but this boy's errand didn't please him. Reluctantly he started for his horse.

"Wait a minute, Walt. We'll take my rig. It'll be handier for bringing things back."

It was Dr. Butler, and Walter was too surprised to answer. He climbed into the buggy beside the physician, wondering why he had chosen to leave the men at this important time.

"What have you been doing since last winter?" Dr. Butler asked as soon as they were out of the yard. "I mean, since Pastor Camp didn't take you back for tutoring?"

64

"Nothing," Walter admitted. "Helping Pa and Gerrit, that's all. Gerrit could have had a lease today and on a good farm, if it wasn't for the quarter sale you were talking about."

"Gerrit will manage," Dr. Butler said. "It's you I'm thinking about. You didn't go back to school, did you?"

"No."

"Who do you think is going to carry on this anti-rent war if none of you from the farms take any real leadership?"

Walter hadn't thought about it.

"The old feudal system can't be ended overnight, Walt," the doctor went on. "It's going to take a couple of years at best just to change the makeup of the legislature. There must be lawyers and educated men representing the farmers in Albany for years to come. In the courts of the state too, after we do get the laws on our side."

He flicked his horse's shanks with a battered whip and went on.

"Pastor Camp's been talking to me. He had reason for feeling he had to listen to Ten Nuys and what the patroon was ordering, right after that 'Indian' raid. But sentiment's changing in town. The storekeeper, the blacksmith, the fellow who runs the apothecary shop all know where their business comes from, and it's the farms. There are only three to eat and be clothed in the Ten Nuys household, unless you count the servants and there's only two of them now."

It was news to Walter. He had felt most of the people in town were on the side of the patroon and against the rough farmers who came in oxcarts, their boots dirty and clothing smelling of the barnyard more often than not.

"Some of you haven't been inside the church since Rent Day." Dr. Butler gave a sidewise glance at Walter. "Try to get your folks to come back, and when they do, you see Pastor Camp about schooling."

Walter knew it wouldn't be hard to get the family back to church. Lucretia had cried when Pa said he wouldn't go again so Gerrit had been taking her almost every Sunday while the others remained at home.

"Boys don't go to school in summer after they're twelve," Walter reminded Dr. Butler. "Even John won't go to common school this summer. He'd old enough to help Pa with the work."

"And young enough to be the one who follows him on the farm," Dr. Butler reminded Walter. "You've got to take a different course. Pastor Camp tells me you should get back at your studies. He . . . maybe I shouldn't say it but I think he has plans for you."

"If you mean the law firm he's connected with in some way, I know about that," Walter said. "He's given the chance to Peter, not me. The storekeeper told me all about it on Rent Day. Peter may have started already, although we saw him in town today."

"He hasn't started and I'm not sure he will," Dr. Butler told Walter. "He wants to stand in well with the patroon and get some job connected with the Van Rensselaer's holdings. He still has the letter, but there are other connections and other ways of getting an education."

"I suppose so, but I still don't see why Pastor Camp had to turn me away," Walter replied. "He was supposed to be pastor of all, not just the Ten Nuys."

Dr. Butler hesitated before he answered. "Pastor Camp wasn't sure what Ten Nuys might be told to do after that raid, Walter. Feeling was high and pressure was put on a lot of us. A man has to think ahead and weigh the outcomes of what he does, or he may make mistakes that will hurt later on."

Walter was sure of that. It was a lesson Pa had tried to impress upon his sons ever since Walter could remember.

"I haven't held it against Pastor Camp too much," Walter

said. "But now I don't see how I could go to school until winter, even if the dominie would take me back."

"Will you see him?" Dr. Butler pressed. "Will you speak to your father about going back to church?"

Walter considered it. Pa had a high regard for Dr. Butler. "Can I tell Pa what you've said?" he asked.

"You can tell him everything I've said."

Walter had an opportunity that very evening after he had delivered the food Ma sent to Mrs. Yates. A cider jug had appeared while he and the doctor were gone and the men were gathered near the fire, shoulder to shoulder, singing. Gerrit's clear tenor rose strong above the others. They were singing a new song that had appeared in the rural sections after a sheriff named Bill Snyder had been turned back by an aroused army of farmers. The words, half belligerent, half humorous, rang out lustily now, the moving shadows of the men flickering in rhythm on the grass.

> "The moon was shining silver bright,
> The sheriff came in the dead of night.
> High on the hill sat an 'Indian' true
> And on his horn a blast he blew.
>
> Keep out of the way, big Bill Snyder.
> Tar your coat and feather your hide, sir!"

With a sense of satisfaction Walter sat on the grass beside his father who was quietly listening. There were two "Indians" here tonight who had not blown their blasts, but the neighbors were not holding it against them. Pa had been the first to offer to tax himself in support of the latest operation Big Thunder was advocating. The Platts were not being shunned tonight, and *belonging* was a comfortable feeling.

Now, while they were quietly watching the others, was a good time to tell Pa of his conversation with Dr. Butler.

"There's a change in sentiment among the townspeople,

Dr. Butler says," Walter began. "More of the merchants are for the farmers."

Pa said "Good!" and tapped his fingers against the soft earth in time with the music. Walter wasn't sure he was paying much attention, but it was easier to talk in the semi-darkness than when Pa's penetrating eyes were on him.

"He thinks Pastor Camp would tutor me again, too."

The tapping stopped. "He told Dr. Butler? Sent word?" Pa sounded incredulous. "You'd like that, wouldn't you?"

"Maybe he could help me decide what I'm to do, Pa," Walter said. "Everyone else seems to know. I'm the odd one."

"It's not you who's odd, it's the way things are," Pa corrected him. "I wanted you to go on with your tutoring. I thought Pastor Camp could help you, too."

It was true. Walter sat quietly and waited.

"Ma hasn't felt right about you and John not going to church," Pa went on, then began tapping with the strident singing again. "We'll go next Sunday and you talk to Pastor Camp after the services."

Walter thought of little else the rest of that week. He wondered if Peter was continuing his studies during the summer. Peter had talked about going to college to take up law, but now he probably had abandoned that plan since he had the letter of recommendation. Peter hadn't cared as much for books as Walter, but he might be tutoring.

Sunday finally came, and Walter felt self-conscious and uncomfortable when he walked with John behind Pa and Ma, Gerrit and Lucretia, into the church. The unadorned walls of the building and the worn plank pews were unchanged, yet they seemed strange. He watched uneasily for the Ten Nuys to appear in their pew in the front of the church. They came late and walked to their accustomed places without looking to right or left. They were the first to leave after Pastor Camp pronounced the final "Amen."

Walter waited in the churchyard while other people visited, catching bits of conversation now and then. A large woman in a black bonnet and wearing a black shawl over her shoulders was telling a few people that Mrs. Ten Nuys' early roses were beginning to bloom. She must be the family servant, Walter thought, and looking at her more closely he recognized the customer who was in the store when he appeared there on Rent Day. Only a few months ago she had heard him admit that Pastor Camp had turned him away. It seemed to Walter that the ladies she was speaking to were not being very cordial. He watched her until Pastor Camp came to him, smiling and with a hand outstretched.

"Walter, I'm glad you and your folks are here today. I've missed you."

"We missed coming, too," Walter admitted honestly.

"Did you go back to school?" Then seeming to sense the answer, "I suppose not, and now you'll be working on the farm all day. Besides, only little tots come to me in the summer."

"I guess that's how it is," Walter agreed.

Pastor Camp lowered his voice. "You can make up what you missed these last three months, if you will." His blue eyes looked troubled, as though he were the one who might be turned aside now, but Walter had no such intention.

"How could I?"

"I'll give you the books and mark out how much you should do each week." Pastor Camp turned his back to the others while he spoke. "I'll write out questions for you and you can bring back the answers each Sunday. You can study at night, can't you?"

It was a generous offer. "I won't be too tired," Walter assured him.

"Then go back into the church. There's a package under the pulpit. I've marked out the first week's lessons and put in the questions. You bring back the answers next week, and I'll have another set for you. By next winter . . . well, we'll wait and see. But for now there's no need for anyone to know about it, except your folks, of course."

He turned from Walter to rejoin the members of his congregation who still were visiting in the churchyard.

The unexpected secrecy surprised Walter. With a feeling of conspiracy he re-entered the empty church. The floor boards creaked loudly under his heavy boots and his hands shook when he took the package from its hiding place. Pastor Camp must still fear the displeasure of the patroon if he had to hide the fact that he was giving Walter a chance to continue his studies. A chance at something more, Walter couldn't help feeling. Hadn't Pastor Camp just hinted? And Dr. Butler too?

The minister was leaving Pa when Walter came out. One glance at the package Walter tried to hide under his arm and Pa started his family toward the waiting wagon. Gerrit and Lucretia already were on their way to her parents' farm.

John spied the package as soon as they were in their seats. "What have you got there?" he demanded.

"Just a book," Walter answered. "I'll show it to you when we get home, if you want to see it."

In the front seat, Ma changed the conversation.

"Drive slow past the rose garden, Pa," she said, straightening her bonnet primly. "Mrs. Ten Nuys had her servant invite some of the town people in after church. I'd like to see how she entertains, even if we weren't invited."

Ma had plenty of opportunity to see the entire expanse of lawn and flowers and hedge that extended from the big stone house to the road. They were directly opposite when a horseman galloped up alongside, pulled to a halt and addressed Pa.

"Are you Gerrit Platt?"

70

"No, I'm his father. You were looking for Gerrit?"

"Yes. I'm Abe Harrison's son-in-law," the man introduced himself. "At church they said Gerrit had gone this way."

Pa explained Gerrit's destination and pointed the direction. "Why do you want him? Has anything happened? Anything serious?"

"Plenty serious," the man said. "Paw Harrison fell and broke a hip last night. I can't do the work for him. I've got my own farm and no help at all. Paw'll fix it so Gerrit gets a fair share if he'll come now and work this summer. If crops are good, it would take care of the quarter sale, maybe."

Walter felt his grip on the package of books tighten. This was Gerrit's chance and he would go. Now with the summer work ahead—cultivating, haying, harvest—Pa would have to rely upon him, from sunup to sundown. He'd be dog tired when it came time to study.

With a sick feeling Walter turned from Abe Harrison's son-in-law to the other side of the road and Mrs. Ten Nuys' rose garden. The servant woman had placed a table beside the trellis and was bringing plates of cakes, but the garden was empty. So far, no one from the church had come.

Then he saw Peter. He was standing by the hedge and in plain sight, had anyone looked in that direction instead of toward the roses. He had heard every word of course, for he was only a few feet away and looking directly at Pa and the messenger Mr. Harrison had sent for Gerrit.

Cautiously Walter moved his arm to cover his package. Had Peter seen that too, and perhaps guessed the contents? Would he care? Would he make trouble?

Chapter 7

Walter never forgot the summer of 1844. He was accustomed to working during every hour of daylight at seeding and harvest time, but this year there was an urgency he had never felt before. Without Gerrit, every minute and every move had to count.

Holding the plow in the earth, avoiding stones and entanglements with buried roots, was hard work. Pa had two good plows with wooden moldboards, the tips fashioned of bog iron taken from the swamp years ago. He and Walter kept them both in use until the earth was turned and ready for the heavy log roller.

They planted oats in early May and later on, buckwheat. By June the winter wheat was an emerald sea waving toward the gray-green foothills of the Catskills off beyond Pa's rolling acres. Devil's paint brush and daisies bloomed in the hay fields, but Walter had no time to think of the lush beauty of summer. When night came and chores were finally done, the Platts were too tired to talk. They ate supper in silence by candlelight, then Pa let Walter stretch out on the floor in front of the open kitchen door and sleep for half an hour while John helped Ma with the household work. John could go to bed after that, but for Walter there were the lessons Pastor Camp mapped out each week. More than once he fell asleep again before he had finished, and too often the questions weren't all answered when he took his report to church to exchange after services for another set of questions.

Walter wasn't sure Pastor Camp would let him come back when the older boys were ready to start in December. When harvest was over, and the wild geese were honking their way south again, he thought about it seriously. It was almost winter. The church was cold, people were bringing their soapstones, and no one was lingering under the bare trees in the church yard as they did in summer.

"Pa, should I ask Pastor Camp about tutoring this winter?" Walter asked on the way to church one chill November morning. "He said 'next winter we'll see.' Do you think sentiment has changed enough now so he can take me openly?"

When Pa was slow to reply, Ma spoke up. "There were few enough ladies in the Ten Nuys' rose gardens after church this summer, if that's any indication. I noticed the servant stopped spreading the table after one or two Sundays."

"I don't know how well you've done with your lessons," Pa finally said. "You've tried hard. We'll not hurry away after church today, even though we'll all be mortal cold. After the others have gone maybe you can have a word with him."

Walter thought more about the answer he might get from Pastor Camp than he did about the sermon that Sunday and he waited, nervous and uncomfortable, while people began shaking the minister's hand and filing out of church. It was a relief when he heard Pastor Camp telling one after another that lessons were starting for the older boys the following week. He was making no distinction between town and farm people and when Pa reached the door he said distinctly, "I hope you're sending Walter."

Foremost in Walter's mind after that was Peter Ten Nuys. How was Peter going to treat him, if they were in the same class again?

Peter wasn't in the pastor's large and somewhat barren living room when Walter was admitted the first day of lessons, but at mid-afternoon there was a knock on the door and before Pastor Camp had greeted him, Peter burst into the room, cheeks red with cold and eyes bright with excitement. When he saw Walter he stopped, his expression changing to one of surprise.

"Yes, Peter, what is it?" Pastor Camp asked.

"I . . . I didn't know you'd enlarged the class," Peter answered, staring openly at Walter. The other boys looked at one another questioningly, shifting in their seats, and for a few moments Walter wondered if they might take sides with Peter and make him unwelcome. But there was an advantage in the fact that Peter had been taken off guard. Obviously he did not know Walter had been studying all summer, making up the lessons he had missed and preparing to resume his work with the others.

"I have a right to continue my education too!" Walter spoke up fearlessly. "We all pay for the support of the church, you know."

"I suppose so," Peter conceded. "It's in your leases. But that's not important now. I've just got back from Albany where we had business with the patroon." He paused to let the boys appreciate the importance of his trip, then handed a newspaper to Pastor Camp. "Just read this!"

"What is it?" the minister asked, needlessly for Peter couldn't wait to talk.

"Dr. Smith Boughton's in jail. Your Big Thunder!"

74

"Big Thunder?" Walter gasped involuntarily.

"Yes, and about time." Peter pulled his coat and hat off and prepared to take his place with the others. "He made a lecture tour through Columbia County but lecturing wasn't enough for him. This time he went too far. At Hudson he was arrested after he and his 'Indians' had prevented a sheriff's sale."

Walter felt as though the entire movement for the farmers had collapsed. Dully he heard Pastor Camp asking what charge had been placed against Dr. Boughton.

"Robbery." Peter sounded triumphant and hurried to explain the circumstances to his open-mouthed audience. "The Sheriff was to sell a farm in Copake but Boughton's gang burned the writs and stopped the sale. Then the sheriff got reinforcements and surprised Big Thunder at Hudson."

Pastor Camp had found the article by that time. Peter watched him closely while he squinted to read the fine print.

"Yes, the farmers threatened to storm the jail," Peter said, anticipating what Pastor Camp was reading. "So the Burgess Corps is there to keep order."

"What do you think is going to happen now?" the minister asked, walking back to the front of the room. Peter sat down apart from the others and stretched his stout legs into the room.

If the news of Dr. Boughton's arrest alarmed the minister he did not show it. When Peter was slow to answer, he repeated the question, straightening his stooped shoulders and looking directly at the would-be representative of the patroon.

"I asked what you think is going to happen now, Peter?"

"In Albany they are saying John Van Buren, son of the last president, will prosecute," Peter told him. "With Mr. Van Buren acting as attorney general I doubt if even your Stanton & Stanton could save Big Thunder."

Walter had never heard of Stanton & Stanton. Could this be the law firm to which Pastor Camp had given Peter a letter?

Pastor Camp ignored his pupil's remark and spreading the paper on the table pointed to another item.

"What do they say in Albany about this state meeting at Berne?" he questioned. "It says here that delegates are to be elected from all the Hudson Valley counties to formulate a plan for carrying on more vigorously than ever. There may be important action taken at Berne, Peter."

Peter shrugged as though to minimize the importance of the Berne meeting, then suddenly straightened in his chair. "Will the Stantons be at Berne?" His voice had changed and a calculating look came over his face fleetingly. Almost too quickly he stretched his legs out again, ignored his own question, and assumed his air of confidence over the turn of events. But Pastor Camp had not missed that half-whispered question. He turned away from the class and his hand was trembling when he took the tongs to place another log on the fire.

"Anyway, with Boughton in jail this revolt is as good as over," Peter resumed. "He'll get a good, long sentence."

"Perhaps I should preach a sermon from Matthew next Sunday," Pastor Camp said quietly. " 'I was a stranger, and ye took me not in: naked, and ye clothed me not: sick, and in prison, and ye visited me not.' "

Peter flushed at the rebuke but he did not answer back, and Pastor Camp turned to his schoolbooks again. Whether Peter was too chagrined to concentrate or whether he had forgotten last year's lessons, Walter could not know but his classmate made a poor showing. His coat was on top of the pile hanging on pegs behind the door and when the lesson ended Peter jerked it on and was gone with an abrupt good-bye while the others were dressing slowly against the cold outside.

Walter fumbled among the garments for his own coat, forced his arms through the twisted sleeves and was about to follow Peter when Pastor Camp motioned him away from the door.

"It would do no good to question Peter, if that's what you have in mind to do," the minister said after the others had gone. "Whatever he intends, he wouldn't tell you."

"But the letter you gave him . . . was it to Stanton & Stanton? Are they your relatives?"

The minister nodded slowly. "More than likely he's right too, and my brother-in-law or my nephew will be at Berne. Since I wrote that letter they've come out against the patroon's title. They're helping the farmers. That's probably the reason Peter isn't reading law with them now."

"But he has the letter!" At the thought of what it might imply Walter's throat tightened. "He could go to Berne and be accepted by your relatives, because you wrote it."

"Don't say it, Walter," the minister admonished wiping a lock of thin hair back from his forehead. "It would be . . . treacherous. Don't accuse him."

Walter could not forget that look on Peter's face, however. Certainly the idea had come to Peter.

"He wouldn't think it was anything but a service to the patroon, if he could find out what the farmers are planning," Walter said. Then, when the minister didn't answer, he continued in a low voice. "Pastor Camp, I took the 'Indian' oath once. It was a pledge to secrecy and to act in any capacity for the good of the tenant farmers. There may be action taken at Berne that the patroons shouldn't know."

Pastor Camp stared into his snow-filled yard. His lips

77

moved but no words came and Walter waited, wondering if he was praying.

"You could write to the Stantons," Walter finally urged. "You could warn them."

"Put in writing an ugly assumption against the son of the patroon's agent and a man who has been my friend, when it may not be true?" Pastor Camp shook his head. "Walter, once I made the mistake of acting as though I were not the shepherd of all my flock. I can't do that again."

The minister lay a kindly hand on Walter's arm. "Don't worry. A way will open to protect the Stantons and Peter too if he is tempted."

Walter left the parsonage with a feeling of foreboding. He dreaded telling Pa and the neighbors of Dr. Boughton's arrest, but before he reached home he learned that the news had preceded him. Tom rode to meet him, urging his uncle's old plow horse to a faster pace than the animal was accustomed to.

"Walt, have you heard?" Tom called.

"Yes, if you mean about Big Thunder," Walter answered. "How did you know?"

"Committee members are out on all roads, calling meetings. You and I are to take these roads. The singing school tomorrow night is to be a meeting of the organization instead. Every man must come."

"What are they to do?" Walter asked.

"Elect a delegate to a big state-wide meeting at Berne. Tomorrow night at your house."

Elect a delegate, and at his house! Someone from his own community would be going to Berne. In that instant Walter knew what he wanted to do. Whoever was elected, he would go with the delegate! There was one sure way to help Pastor Camp and keep Peter from "yielding to temptation" as the minister had put it. Walter must go to Berne.

The merrymaking that had been intended for the following night was forgotten by the men who crowded into the Platt parlor. Walter and Tom sat on the stairs between the kitchen and large front room and listened while once more Sam Yates took charge.

"Before this calamity happened, plans had been started for a great state-wide meeting January 15 and 16 in the Lutheran Church in Berne," he began. "That's the biggest meeting place in these parts. Now we must go there and show that we're not licked. We must find out whether we should free Boughton by force, or how to help him."

The suggestion that plans might be made at Berne for freeing, or even defending Dr. Boughton, strengthened Walter's decision. Whatever took place at Berne, no Benedict Arnold should learn of it, and through Pastor Camp too, when Walter could prevent it.

Peering around the edge of the doorway Walter saw rows of grim faces in the candlelight. Once in awhile someone asked a question but for the most part they listened in silence while Sam told what he knew of the forthcoming convention. There wasn't much discussion of who would be the official delegate. Walter had wished it might be Pa, but Sam Yates had been more active and the vote for him was unanimous.

After the men had gone, Walter told Pa of his fears and his plan for forestalling any action by Peter at the Berne convention. They were putting the parlor to rights while Ma was busy in the kitchen clearing away the food that was left from the lunch she had served, and Pa listened without interrupting.

"It could happen," he agreed when Walter finished talking. "And Peter could justify it to himself I suppose."

He sat down heavily on the old setee and motioned Walter to a chair.

"We've known about that letter for a long time, Walt," he said, staring into the smouldering ashes in the fireplace. "Ever since that Rent Day when you went to town with me and the storekeeper told us. I'd hoped Pastor Camp might give you that opportunity, but Ten Nuys asked for it and the dominie couldn't refuse."

"You'd hoped I'd get it?" Walter could scarcely believe it. He had thought Pastor Camp would help him to get into some occupation besides farming, but he had never dreamed of going away to read law.

Pa nodded. "It was the chance I wanted for you," he admitted. "Pastor Camp knew that, when I eked out the money to pay for tutoring instead of sending you to the common school. Ten Nuys knew it too. So if you should go to Berne you musn't try to find the minister's relatives and say anything to them against Peter. It would only react against you. You could be wrong, too, as Pastor Camp told you."

"I could keep my eye on Peter, if he should go there." Walter insisted. "Why, I wouldn't let him out of my sight if he came to Berne! I could let everyone know which side he's on."

"Let's wait and see what happens between now and January," Pa advised. "Maybe Peter won't go and you can be sure of it, some way. I . . . I just wish it didn't have to be *you* who'll go to Berne."

"But I want to go!" Walter told his father. "I'd like to go even if there wasn't any danger Peter will turn spy. I want to see how a great meeting is conducted."

"Well, let's not say anything to Sam Yates yet," Pa suggested.

Walter waited with mounting excitment as the days passed. Neither Pastor Camp nor Peter mentioned the anti-rent convention again, but nothing else was talked about wherever farmers gathered. At the store in town, after church, over the fence rows between their fields they speculated and exchanged views, and Walter listened. Then, two days before the convention, Gerrit unexpectedly rode into the yard.

"I've come to ask a favor, Pa," he said, dismounting and leading his horse to the barn with Pa and Walter alongside. "Old Mr. Harrison was elected alternate to the Berne convention, as an honor because of the work he's done in the past in Schoharie County. But now it's developed that he's the one to go, for the delegate can't. I'll have to drive him and take care of the horses. I wondered if Walt could come and stay with Lucretia and Mrs. Harrison while I'm gone. The barn chores are too much for them."

Walter's heart sank. Pa would welcome this turn of events.

"There might be a bad storm too," Walter heard his father saying. "You'd better to, Walt. You can trust Gerrit to carry on with what you had in mind, if need be. You can tell him on the way to his place, after we've had something to eat."

Chapter 8

Walter had not seen the Harrison farm since the day he and Gerrit had gone to look it over. He remembered the old couple well, but in the winter twilight, with great drifts of snow banked against the house and barns, the buildings looked smaller and more huddled into the earth than he remembered them. Lights were bright in the windows, however, and gray smoke reaching skyward from the chimney promised warmth and cheer. Then there would be baby Elias, now more than a year old, and Walter smiled to himself at the thought of his nephew. This would be a pleasant change, even though he couldn't go to Berne. He whistled while he helped unharness the horses and followed Gerrit to the stanchions, where cows stomped and chewed their cuds, with a sense of pleasant anticipation. When they finally went to the house, each carrying a milk bucket, the chores were finished.

Gerrit opened the kitchen door and called "Hello." The voice that answered wasn't Lucretia's. It was full and deep-throated and vibrant.

"Surprise, Brother Gerrit!"

"Susan!" For a moment Gerrit stood in the open doorway, looking his astonishment. "Susan, you haven't met my brother Walter. This is Lucretia's younger sister, Walt."

Walter set the milk bucket down to take the hand that was offered in friendly greeting, while Gerrit closed the door on the cold of the outer shed.

Susan, who appeared about Walter's age, was as different from Lucretia as opposites could be. Her eyes were blue, but the brows and lashes that set them off were almost black. She had fair hair too, with the gold in it so deep that it seemed copper-colored in the flickering candlelight. Her heavy curls were tied at the back of her neck with a bright red bow, instead of the black velvet Lucretia usually wore. Each feature was strong and distinctly carved.

"We thought you'd never get home," Susan was saying. "Come, put the milk here and get washed for supper. Lucretia's putting a fresh dress on the baby. They'll be down in a minute."

"It's plain to see you've been busy," Gerrit said looking approvingly at the kitchen table, cheerful with a red and white cover and dishes gleaming in the soft light. In the center a big pitcher held sprigs of waxed autumn leaves and rich brown cattails. "I can always tell when Susan's come, Walt," he went on. "Something new here, something to brighten the place up."

Lucretia came into the room then, Elias in her arms, and she too looked different than Walter remembered her. She had fluffed her own hair becomingly and had a smile for her husband when she handed his kicking, laughing son to him.

"Walter, it's nice to have you here," Lucretia welcomed him. "If I'd known Susan was coming we wouldn't have gone for you. Susan can manage anything."

"Well, almost anything," Susan smiled. "Anything I've ever found on a farm, let's say."

83

Walter could believe it. She wasn't a large or ungainly girl, but she was well-built and her laughing eyes were fearless.

"I'm glad to meet my new brother-in-law," Susan went on. "Lucretia and I could have managed though. We have before. I just tell her what to do and she does it!"

Confidence rang in her voice and laughter, and there was understanding in the look she gave her older sister. "Call the Harrisons for supper, Lou."

Walter had never seen a girl like Susan. She moved quickly from the fireplace to the table with food for the evening meal, the heaping platters smelling so good that little Elias extended both hands and yelled with anticipation. Her eyes were quick to see that the candles were moved so they lighted the entire table, to find the baby's bib. She had a hand for the old couple too, when they came into the room. Then she turned to Gerrit.

"I'll feed the baby tonight. You have the chore every night."

Elias went to her instantly and she propped him on her lap with assurance. "Down with your little hands now, while Papa says Grace," she murmured and for a moment the child obeyed.

Sitting opposite her through that pleasant meal, hearing the praise Lucretia gave unstintingly, a thought for himself kept forcing its way into Walter's mind. Why couldn't he go to Berne with Gerrit and Mr. Harrison? Lucretia couldn't have cared for the baby, the elderly lady, and the farm animals alone, but now Susan was here. She had brightened the appearance of the house, cooked the evening meal, and even cheered Lucretia into prettying herself and joining in the atmosphere of gaiety.

When the talk turned to the next day's trip and the excitement of the great anti-rent convention in Berne, she seemed to sense what was in Walter's mind. Quite suddenly she put her fork down to look at him forthrightly.

"I'll wager you'd like to go to Berne too," she said. "If I were a man, nothing could keep me away."

"You have to be a delegate to go," Lucretia reminded her. "Or be taking someone with business there, as Gerrit is doing."

"Hundreds of people will be in Berne who aren't delegates!" Susan scoffed. "Everybody for miles around will be listening at the doors and waiting at the inn to hear what happened the minute the delegates come out."

Walter wanted to agree with her, but he was reluctant to press his own cause. He looked across the table at Gerrit who was considering her words carefully. Gerrit knew how badly Walter wanted to go, even if he hadn't felt an obligation to protect Pastor Camp against any misguided act on Peter's part.

Unexpectedly Mr. Harrison decided the question. "Of course the boy wants to go," the elderly man said. His voice trembled but his eyes were bright and alert: "What red-blooded young man wouldn't? These are the 'embattled farmers' again, ready as they were at Lexington. There won't be any rooms at the inn, but the relatives Gerrit and I will stay with can find a spot somewhere under the roof for one more."

Walter looked across the table to see Susan beaming, even while she held the baby's hands back from his plate of food.

"I certainly thank everybody," Walter said looking straight at her. "I wanted to go to Berne more than I've ever wanted anything I can remember."

He hoped she would know he was thanking her most of all, even though he didn't say it. He was sure she did, for the same understanding look she had given Lucretia shone in her eyes when she smiled back at him.

January's snow was deep and cold on the rock-studded, flat-top chain of hills stretching into the Schoharie Valley when Gerrit and Walter and Mr. Harrison drove into Berne. Ice gleamed from shore to shore on Werner's Lake.

"Berne was named for the Swiss city," Mr. Harrison explained, his teeth chattering and his breath freezing in the winter air. "The Foxenkill's right pretty in summer, and that's Grippy Hill and Irish Hill you see in the background. We're at the highest point in the Helderbergs, but you can have the scenery. I can't get to a good fire soon enough."

"It'll probably be warm in more ways than one where you'll be soon," Walter suggested. "If I hear anything before the meetings let out, I'll have to stay in the cold and listen at the door."

"Drive the sleigh up close to one of the windows if you can, Gerrit," Mr. Harrison directed. "That way you may be able to see a little. Hear too, if they open the window for a breath of air."

The brick church loomed ahead, its square white steeple shining in the winter sunshine. It was early in the morning but already there were rigs in the churchyard; Walter did not see any he recognized as belonging to the Ten Nuys, however. When Gerrit maneuvered his sleigh beside one of the windows it was to claim the last preferred space. Mr. Harrison gave directions for taking the horses to his relative's stables and after Gerrit left with them Walter helped the stiff old man up the slippery steps and into the church.

One glimpse of the big auditorium was all Walter got. The church was filling with delegates. They stood in the aisles and crowded at the back, with more men arriving constantly to push their way inside. Walter could see little except broad backs and shifting shoulders. He stood inside the door with Mr. Harrison as long as he dared, enjoying the warmth of the building, listening to every word, and watching for Sam Yates.

"That's Dr. Frederick Crounse," Mr. Harrison whispered pointing to one man just ahead. "He may be chairman of this meeting. He was chairman back in 1839 when the first anti-rent movement started right here in Berne."

Walter stretched his neck to get a glimpse of the man, but Mr. Harrison was prodding him to look in the opposite direction. "That's Hugh Scott," he said pointing to another. "He's from Westerlo and was secretary back in '39. You're getting to see the leaders, anyway."

Walter was grateful for that one hasty glimpse. Later when he was standing in his sleigh outside, pressing his face against the window, he could identify the men who were presiding.

The churchyard was full of people trying to see and hear, speculating on action that might be taken and candidates to be endorsed. Every rig under the four church windows on either side of the building was soon filled, and men who had never seen each other before were telling their names and where they were from, and passing on bits of information to each other. Still Walter did not see Peter.

"Who is chairman, can you tell?" a young man called to Walter. "It's important."

"It's Dr. Crounse," Walter replied, proud that he could recognize the leader. "Climb on up! There's room in our sleigh."

When the stranger did not immediately land beside him Walter glanced down and at once regretted his careless invitation. A heavy, built-up boot on one foot made climbing difficult for this man. At once Walter leaned over the side of the sleigh and extended a hand.

"This way. Up on the tongue," he directed.

A grateful nod answered him and the young man soon was pressing against the side of the church and peering in as intently as the others.

"That's William Murphy of New Scotland acting as secretary," the newcomer explained. "Hugh Scott must have been elected to some office or he wouldn't be up in front. It's a conservative group that has the meeting in charge."

Walter had understood from the talk at home that anti-renters were progressives and he looked at his companion questioningly. He was a slender young man of about twenty-five years, whose deep hazel eyes were unusually large and intense. His forehead was high, his nose thin, and heavy sideburns along his cheeks accentuated the long oval of his serious face. From the style and nature of his clothing Walter did not think he came from the farms. Many who crowded about the church appeared to be merchants or professional people.

"Should the conservatives be in charge of this meeing?" Walter asked, hoping to draw him out.

"Yes indeed!" The young man fairly snapped the words out and his jaw set in a determined manner. Then he glanced at Walter and spoke less vehemently. "These farmers must adopt sensible resolutions and show themselves responsible if they want the support of men like John Young and Ira Harris. I wish we could hear, but there's too much noise in this yard for us to catch a word, even if they opened a window."

When he crowded nearer Walter stepped back to let him have the place closest to the window and at that instant Gerrit touched Walter's arm. Following his brother's eyes Walter saw Peter riding into the churchyard.

"Let me be the one," Walter said quickly and before Gerrit could answer he jumped from the sleigh and walked to the hitching post where Peter was tying his horse. Peter hadn't seen him, and the advantage gave Walter a feeling of self-confidence. He was surprised at the assurance in his voice when he spoke.

"Hello, Peter."

The land agent's son dropped the reins at the greeting and whirled quickly, a look of alarm on his face.

"What are you doing here?" Peter demanded, then reached to recover the lines from the snow at his feet.

"Watching the proceedings from a good seat at one of the church windows," Walter replied. "There's room for you in our sleigh."

"Thanks, but I have friends here," Peter answered recovering from his surprise. "I'll be all right."

"You have friends at *this* meeting?" Walter questioned. "Perhaps they have a better spot than we. Do you mind if I come along with you?"

Peter frowned and didn't reply. He tied his horse slowly and securely as though waiting for Walter to go. Finally he straightened up.

"Don't you wait for people to invite you to join them?" He spoke with the old note of arrogance and started to walk away.

"This time, no," Walter said firmly and stepped to Peter's side, determined to stay with him wherever he went. For the first time in his life Walter felt that he, not Peter, had the upper hand. This crowd at Berne—all friends of the fighting farmers—would thank him for curbing Peter's activities if they knew a representative of the patroon was here for any reason. Walter felt sure of Peter's intentions too, not only from the first guilty look but from his eagerness to be rid of Walter.

Peter went no farther. "Walter Platt, I didn't come here to see you and you know it. And I want no bodyguard."

He stood near the hitching rail, feet apart, a picture of belligerence.

"Nevertheless, you're going to have one if you stay," Walter said. "This isn't a meeting of the patroon's men and you're the one who wasn't invited."

"It happens I have business here." Peter's eyes flashed with anger.

"Could it be with Stanton & Stanton?" Walter asked.

The name of the law firm sent the color from Peter's ruddy face. He raised a clenched fist as though to strike and Walter stepped aside quickly, out of range of the blow he expected. If they fought Peter might win once more, but he would attract a great deal of attention.

"I could bash your face in," Peter muttered. "I've a mind to do it, too."

"You'll have an audience if you try it," Walter reminded him. "They'll want to know who you are and why you're here, and I'm not going to keep quiet on the first score. You can answer for the second."

Peter rubbed his clenched fists together and the look he gave Walter was one of hatred.

"Stay if you want to Peter, but you aren't going to be alone one minute," Walter told him. "If you came to spy and betray Pastor Camp, you won't succeed."

Walter expected Peter to deny the accusation but instead he turned to the yard and the milling men and crowded rigs. The spectators nearest to the boys were moving closer to see whether a fight developed, and Walter was sure Peter did not welcome the attention he was already receiving. He looked from rig to rig as though searching for someone, walked a few steps for a better view of the church, then returned to the hitching post, Walter at his side.

"You realize, of course, how insulting you've been?" Peter demanded, chin tilted upward and jaw set.

"If I'm wrong, yes," Walter admitted. "But do you expect me to believe any associate of the patroon came to this meeting honorably?"

Walter had taken no pains to lower his voice and the questioning looks of the men around the hitching post could not have been reassuring to Peter.

"There's nothing I can do with a sneak at my heels, and this is your crowd, I admit." He muttered the words, untied his horse and rode away without another look at Walter.

Walter watched him with relief rather than any sense of victory. Accusing Peter and defying him had not been pleasant, for Walter could recall the days when they had played together as boys in the churchyard at home. Their first fight had ended in an act of generosity on Peter's part, but there probably would have been no such outcome had they turned to fisticuffs today. Actually, their relationship had been strained ever since the night Peter had recognized Gerrit at the land office. It was out in the open now.

Walter stuffed his hands in his pockets and started toward the sleigh, to meet Gerrit coming toward him.

"I'm going to get one of the horses and follow him a mile or so," he said. "It's cold standing in that sleigh anyway, and not very exciting."

It hadn't proved interesting, but Walter went back to the church window. When he jumped into the sleigh he was greeted with unexpected acclaim.

"You took care of that neatly, I must say," the young man he had helped earlier in the day said. He was looking at Walter seriously, and without smiling. "Your brother had all of us ready to pounce if you needed help."

"Gerrit told you who he was?" Walter asked.

"The son of one of the Van Rensselaers' agents," the young man said holding out his hand. "I'm Charles Stanton."

For a moment Walter was speechless, but he took the hand and managed to introduce himself.

Walter's name meant nothing to Charles Stanton and he turned back to his lookout post.

"Have you a decent place to sleep tonight?" he asked while he peered through the window. "I have a room at the in and I'd be glad to share it with you."

It was a generous offer, but Walter hesitated to accept. A meeting with the Stanton's was what Pa had warned against. He was still trying to think how he could decline without seeming unappreciative when Stanton took a firm grip on the side of the sleigh and clumsily got out.

"They're breaking up," he said. "I'll expect you at the inn tonight."

In spite of his handicap, the young lawyer was at the door of the church as soon as it opened and was lost in the crowd at once. Walter found Mr. Harrison and walked with him to his friend's home where Gerrit was waiting in the warm kitchen. Briefly he told his brother who Charles Stanton was, and of his invitation.

"I'd go," Gerrit advised. "This house and every other place in Berne is overcrowded. "You'll sleep on the floor here. Between 150 and 200 delegates have come to this convention and Mr. Harrison isn't the only one who brought other people along. Besides, with all the talk on what's happened at the meeting, nobody is going to think of anything else."

If the church had been crowded that day, the inn was more so at night. Men jammed in the hall, stood in groups in the parlors on one side and the barroom on the other, some smoking and drinking and all talking at once. They sat on the stairway leading to the second floor, or pushed their way from group to group. No one paid any attention to Walter, and the heavy tobacco smoke dimmed the wavering candle light until it was difficult to recognize anyone at the far end of either hall or barroom. The parlors, where there were chairs and setees, were too crowded for anyone to even try to enter.

For a few minutes Walter surveyed the place. He had never been in a tavern before. On the walls, advertising signs announced the schedule of stagecoach routes, and of the *Constitution* and *Constellation,* Hudson River steamboats plying between New York and Albany.

From the bedlam of conversation Walter learned little, although a few men did talk to him. They quoted the Declaration of Independence, likened the landlords to King George III, and predicted the next day's events. Hugh Scott, Walter learned, had been named president of the convention and he and Dr. Crounse had taken the lead in disavowing the use of force against lawful authority, abandoning disguises, and declaring the ballot to be the weapon of the organization from now on.

Walter finally spied Charles Stanton and the lawyer's nod told him he had been seen. It was late in the evening, however, before Stanton motioned him to the stairs and they went to the bedroom on the floor above. Two small cots had been crowded into the room so they knew they would not be alone.

"We'll take the bed," Stanton announced, sitting down on the blue and white handwoven counterpane, and motioning Walter to the one chair in the room. "Tell me, what did you think of the day's work as you heard of it?"

"The most I learned was that the convention is being guided by cautious men," Walter answered. "That will please my father."

93

"It will get the support of those who can win for the farmers," Stanton said, taking off his coat. "One of the ablest is John Young. If you've wondered why I'm here, it's to let people know Livingston County should keep him in Albany as their assemblyman. He's been working shrewdly since 1843 and he's now the best parliamentarian in the legislature. He knows what he's doing."

"Perhaps Mr. Harrison knows people over there," Walter suggested. "He's been working in the movement for years. My brother Gerrit is old enough to vote but he doesn't live in Livingston County."

"They can spread the word," Mr. Stanton said. "So can you, even if you aren't old enough to vote." He was looking at Walter intently again, without a smile or any trace of real warmth. "What are your plans for the future, young man? You showed yourself level-headed and fearless today. Have you ever thought of studying the law?"

The question came as a complete surprise, and once more Walter found himself unable to answer Charles Stanton readily. How could he admit he had thought of the legal profession? It was Peter who had been promised the opportunity to read law with Stanton & Stanton, and he had kept Peter from seeing the lawyer today. How could he say one word on his own behalf now?

Walter stared at his hands, his mind fumbling for an honorable answer, and the lawyer turned from him to stretch out on the bed with a sigh.

"I can see you haven't," he said. "It's no easy road to travel, but you farmers need to have your own men in Albany."

There was no opportunity for Walter to answer, if indeed there was anything he could say. The men who were to share the room came stumbling in to bed. Long after the others were sleeping soundly Walter lay, stiff and tense, in the bed with Charles Stanton thinking of what he might have said; how he could have answered.

In the morning there was a rush for breakfast and then for the church. Walter thanked his host for the night's hospitality and rejoined Gerrit and Mr. Harrison in the crowded kitchen where they had eaten the day before.

Walter did not see Mr. Stanton again until late in the afternoon and Peter did not reappear. Stanton was moving from one group to another in the churchyard and Walter could guess at his business. From his lookout post in the sleigh Walter had spied Sam Yates and when the delegates filed out he pressed through the pushing men to the side of his neighbor.

"Tell me what happened," Walter urged. "This was the final day."

"We're demanding revocation of the special rights by which landlords name judges and prosecutors and jury so they control the courts," Mr. Yates explained, puffing as he hurried to keep up with the others. "We want the rents we pay taxed. The landlords should pay taxes too. And we want to challenge their title of ownership to the land and all the improvements we've made on it! That's the way to break the old leases."

The men all around them were talking eagerly, enthusiastically. Assurance and victory were in the air, and the names of the men who could win for the farmers were on every tongue.

"Things will be better for you and Tom and Gerrit," Mr. Yates said, slapping Walter on the shoulder. "We old fellows can depend on you to keep up the fight as long as need be. Until we win every point."

Walter heard the same thought voiced on the cold ride back to the Harrison farm. There must be young men prepared to serve in the legislature, educated for positions in the courts, after the farmers' demands had been won. There must be more men like John Young, who, Mr. Harrison said, had worked on his father's farm until he was of age, then had supported himself by teaching school while he studied law in the office of Augustus Bennett of East Avon. Charles Stanton had done his work well, Walter thought.

The exciting events at Berne began to fade into the back of Walter's mind when once more he saw the cluster of Harrison farm buildings, the bare orchard trees and the stark maple sugarbush at the back of the fields. Gerrit hadn't negotiated a sale of the lease to this farm, Walter had learned, but not because he and Mr. Harrison hadn't come to terms. They both hoped for action from the next legislature which would invalidate the quarter sale price, if not overthrow the entire obnoxious system. In the meantime Gerrit and Lucretia continued to carry on the work with a fair division of the proceeds for their labor.

It was Susan that Walter was thinking of, more than Lucretia and Gerrit or even baby Elias, when they drove into the yard. Certainly she would not have left before they returned. He was eager to see her once more and learn more about her. What had she been dong, all her years at home? What would she think if she knew of the ambition that was growing in his mind. And was she really as vibrant with warm friendship, as beautiful in her own sure way, as she had seemed when he met her, only four days before?

Walter had his answer when the sleigh drew to a stop at the woodshed to let Mr. Harrison out before Walter and Gerrit went on to the barn and its chores. The door opened and Susan hurried out, pulling her mittens on as she came. Apparently she had been watching for them, for her warm red scarf was wrapped around her head and neck and she was wearing her coat and heavy boots.

"Gerrit! Mr. Harrison! Go inside and try to reassure Mrs. Harrison and Lou," she directed. "They're both upset. I'll help Walter."

Her voice and anxious expression gave them all concern.

"What's the matter?" Gerrit asked, helping Mr. Harrison out of the sleigh. "What happened?"

"A posse of deputies was here this afternoon," she began. "Already there's talk of reprisals for this Berne meeting. The men said they were going to search the place for 'Indian' disguises, but Mrs. Harrison recognized one of them as a member of Osman Steele's force from over in Delaware County. We told them they couldn't search in Schoharie County. We stood in the door and blocked them and they went away, but when they went, Mrs. Harrison's courage went too. As for Lucretia—well, you know Lou."

Mr. Harrison already was tottering to the woodshed door, Gerrit behind him. Together Susan and Walter drove the horses the short distance to the barn.

"Is Lucretia pretty upset?" Walter asked, trying to keep the disquiet out of his own voice.

"She's almost hysterical and no one but Gerrit can quiet her, if he can," she answered. "Little Elias started crying when he heard his mother sobbing." She shook her head. "Poor Lucretia."

"This isn't good news," Walter admitted. "She's going to worry from now on, particularly every time Gerrit moves off the place."

"She will," Susan agreed. Then, "You know what I think I'll do? There's to be a teachers' institute in this county in another week, because the common school is closed for lack of a teacher. If I can pass the test maybe I can get the position. Then I'd be here to bolster her up, part of the time at least."

"Can you teach?" Her plan surprised Walter, although

when he thought about it he knew he should not have been surprised.

"I don't know," Susan admitted honestly. "I never had a chance to go beyond common school. The first Normal School in the state only opened at Albany last year. But if I can pass the test I don't see why I couldn't do it."

The horses were unhitched and nudged into their stalls without any more words between Walter and Susan. While he pitched fresh hay down from the mows she gathered milk buckets and stools, ready to share in the evening chores.

"You'll pass the test," Walter assured her when he took the bucket she handed him. "It will be a comfort to Gerrit to have you here and . . . well, I'll like knowing where you are. I'd thought perhaps I'd stay over a day or two. There might have been a singing school or something we could go to. But now . . ."

"Now, you'd better get home and see what's happening there," Susan agreed. "This reprisal talk may be just Steele's idea. Mrs. Harrison says he's been a hard man. But we can't tell yet. Anyway, you can come again."

"Yes, I'll come again," Walter promised. He knew he would, but he knew too that if widespread agitation started as a result of the Berne meeting, Peter Ten Nuys would not be satisfied unless he had a part in it.

Chapter 9

Walter returned home to find that once more his story had preceeded him. Fear of reprisals followed quickly on the heels of the convention. Mr. Yates had called another township meeting to report the action at Berne and to warn the farmers to be on the alert. They were pledged not to use disguises, but they could resist forced sales by hiding their cattle and horses if the sheriff appeared on any country road. There were deep woods, tree-covered ravines, and caves on many of the farms.

An uneasy peace settled over pastures and woodlots and farmlands as winter gave way to spring. In March Dr. Boughton was tried, the jury disagreed, and the court released him, giving his followers new heart, but men did their work with an ear attuned for the tin horn that might call them to help one another. In Walter's community Derick Ten Nuys took no action to collect unpaid rents for the patroon. Peter gave up his studies with no explanation to Pastor Camp except "business in Albany" and without his needling the sheriff led no raids. Word of the worsening situation in Delaware County, however, passed from one stone fencerow to the next, whenever a farmer returned from the store or blacksmith shop in town.

"Pa, I can't help worrying about Gerrit and Lucretia and the baby," Walter finally said when Tom came back with these reports. It was a rainy day in early August and they were sharpening scythes and repairing haying tools in the barn. Beyond the open door a gray drizzle veiled their fields and hid the outline of the breadloaf hills beyond. "If this weather keeps up can I ride over tomorrow and see if everything's all right with them?"

"I'd feel better if you did," Pa answered at once. "So would Ma. They're right on the edge of Delaware County and the reputation of that undersheriff Osman Steele isn't getting any better."

Walter started early the next morning. The rain ended before he reached the Harrison farm and all along the road men were out with pitchforks to air and dry their rows of rain-drenched hay or grain. John would be helping Pa with the same task at home and Gerrit would be glad for a hand tomorrow if Walter decided to stay over, as he knew he would.

Walter could see the Harrison buildings for the distance of half a mile and from the moment he glimpsed them he had a premonition all was not well. Six or eight horses were tethered under the trees in the yard and Walter immediately urged his tired animal to increased speed. This could be no meeting of the neighbors. He had seen them in their fields at work.

Before he turned from the main road into the driveway Walter heard Lucretia's hysterical screams.

"Go away! Go away!" She was sobbing and her voice, high-pitched with terror, sent a chill through Walter.

"Gerrit! Gerrit! Help!"

She was answered by a gruff male order to shut up.

"We come to search this place fer disguises," Walter heard a man announce. "You jest keep yer perty mouth closed or we may have to shut it fer ye."

Walter jumped from his horse and raced toward the kitchen door.

"If you're Osman Steele's deputies you have no right . . ." It was Susan but sounding more frightened than authoritative. Then came the anguished wail from the baby.

"You devil! You stepped on his hand!" Lucretia shrieked the word again. "Devil! Devil!"

"Keep him out of the way. He ain't hurt. Neither is this perty one."

Walter reached the kitchen door in time to see one of the men grab Susan by the wrist. Her heavy mass of gold curls flew back from her head as she jerked away.

"I'll take a kiss and ferget the disguise," the man said, a grin spreading over his grimy, be-whiskered face and he tried to pull Susan toward him. She had a baking pan in her hand and with all her force she began beating him about the head while Lucretia increased her cries for help and Elias howled.

Walter swung with all his force and the man reeled and fell to the floor, his head striking against the edge of the kitchen table when he went down. He lay still and for a moment there was silence in the room execept for the baby's sobs.

"You've killed him!" one of the man's companions muttered, staring at the body on the kitchen floor.

Walter was too blinded by rage to believe the accusation or to care.

"Do you want to be next?" he demanded. "Susan, get to the dinner bell and ring it hard."

She started for the kitchen door and another ruffian, cursing, grabbed her and held her back. The man was too large for Walter to manage but he rushed at him and sunk his teeth into the bare arm that held Susan. In another instant Susan was free, but a blow sent Walter spinning across the room. Another pelt floored him, but he knew the fight was over. Susan had the bell ringing wildly.

"Gerrit! Gerrit!" Lucretia's cries came from a long way off. The floor boards moved crazily before Walter's dizzy eyes and something wet and soft and not like sweat trickled over his lips. Blood . . . his own blood. . . . Soft blackness enveloped him.

When he opened his eyes the room was filled with men— quiet men who were not cursing or shouting or leering.

"Walt, are you all right?"

Walter blinked back the fog and his eyes focused on Gerrit's massive shoulders. Cold, wet towels felt good on his throbbing head and the bitter-sweet fragrance of smelling salts was clearing his brain.

"I'm all right." He stretched his arms and legs and felt the kitchen floor boards hard and safe beneath him.

"You came at the right time, boy." It was Mr. Harrison's tremulous voice. Walter turned to speak to him but the movement set his head pounding and he shut his eyes.

"It was Walter's presence of mind that saved us," he heard Susan saying. "I was too scared to think of the dinner bell."

There were other voices then—voices of men Walter didn't know. He lay with his eyes shut, remembering what had happened, while the pain quieted and he began breathing easily again. He moved slightly and looked toward the table where he had last seen another lying motionless. No one was there.

"It was Steele's men all right," Walter heard Gerrit saying. "We can't let this go on. It's not the first time they've forayed out of their own county. But when they attack women and children . . . !"

"There're 1,000 men in the Delaware 'Indian' companies now," someone else said. "Everybody. Old, middle-aged, young. Rich and poor, influential and obscure. It's time they got help from some of the rest and I'm ready to join them the next time Steele makes a move." The voice was gruff and angry.

"So am I!"

"And I."

"The devils! The very devils! Count me in." It was Gerrit, intense and bitter.

"If you mean it, you won't have long to wait," Mr. Harrison said knowingly, and Walter propped himself up on an elbow, pushing the wet towels from his eyes to see what was going on. The kitchen was filled with farmers and others stood in the doorway, rakes and pitchforks in their hands. Susan and Lucretia and the baby had disappered but Walter could hear their footsteps overhead.

"Osman Steele tried to sell Moses Earle's stock for Charlotte Verplanck, the landowner, on July 29th but the Delaware 'Indians' kept anyone from bidding," Mr. Harrison went on. "Steele put the sale off until August 7th and that's tomorrow."

He lowered his voice when he said the word *tomorrow*.

"The statute of distress provides that a sale must be held within five days if it's postponed, doesn't it?" Gerrit asked.

"Yes, but Osman Steele's going to hold it tomorrow just the same. What's the law to him? He makes his own and the courts and the patroon back him up."

For a few minutes there was no sound in the kitchen except the loud ticking of the mantle clock. In the yard outside summer katydid calls mingled with the bell notes of robins and orioles. Then Mr. Harrison spoke again, his quaking voice almost a whipser.

"They've gone back to disguises in Delaware. It's against the pledge made at Berne, but nobody foresaw this situation last January."

"They can use help in Delaware all right."

Walter looked from one grim face to another. He had never seen Gerrit's neighbors before. Bitterness and determination and smothered fury was what he saw. The exchange of looks, the nods and unspoken words were eloquent as they picked up rakes and farming tools. They would join the Delaware "Indians" tomorrow and they would be disguised.

"Spread the word tonight," Mr. Harrison said when one by one they left. "I'm too decrepit to go with you, but by Heaven, if I could I'd be there."

"We'll all meet by the big boulder in the hollow."

When they had gone Walter got unsteadily to his feet. "What happened to the one I knocked down?" he asked. "I guess he wasn't dead, after all."

"Stunned for a few minutes, same as you," Gerrit told him. He ran his fingers through his heavy hair and sat down on one of the ladder-back chairs in the kitchen. "I'm glad I didn't leave my disguise back in Pa's old stone fence," he added.

"What about me?" Walter asked. "Would one of Mrs. Harrison's old wrappers be big enough to cover me?"

"Not you," Gerrit said quickly. "You know how Pa feels."

"If Pa'd been here today to see what I saw, he'd feel differently," Walter insisted. "Anyway, it's all I can do to fight this tyranny."

Gerrit would know what Walter meant. He could not have forgotten the strange circumstances at Berne, and the opportunity to fight more effectively for the farmers that had been within Walter's reach. Walter's hands gripped the back of a kitchen chair as he steadied himself and across the Harrison kitchen his eyes met Gerrit's. Mr. Harrison, watching, got up and started for the floor above.

"There'll be a disguise, come morning," he said and tottered away.

In spite of his aching head, which throbbed throughout the evening, Walter went to sleep early and slept soundly. He awakened with an unexplainable sense of satisfaction, only to realize that the day was just beginning and the blow he would strike for freedom was still ahead.

Gerrit and Mr. Harrison were up, and the chores done when Walter went into the barnyard. Mr. Harrison smiled grimly and pointed to the calico wrapper and sheepskin mask hanging on a peg beside the harnesses. In a roll on the floor was Gerrit's old bundle.

"Now I wonder where these things came from?" the old man said facetiously. "Maybe you'd better get them out of here, in case another searching party shows up."

Gerrit smiled at the joke and Walter rolled his disguise into a small bundle. It was time to start.

The appointed meeting place was deep in a valley where the road twisted between steep-rising, wooded hills. Gerrit and Walter had seemed to be riding alone until they made a sudden turn and came upon the bare rock jutting grotesquely from the lush growth of seedling trees and bushes. It was at a crossroads and from all four directions men suddenly appeared, some already masked. A horseman in a scarlet disguise with a black military cap and red mask, seemed to be the leader. He held up his hand for silence.

"If any of you don't know the story of this sale, a levy has been made on four horses, six cows, and eight hogs to settle for back rent of only $64!" He waited for the injustice of it to be recognized. Why, a span of horses alone was worth $100, Walter knew.

"Peter Wright, the law agent for Charlotte Verplanck, and Sheriff Moore are at the Earle farm now, but the 'Indians' have kept them from starting the sale so far," the leader went on. "Both sides are expecting reinforcements. Wright was trying to recognize the 'Indians' this morning, so keep your masks on. He's been told he'll go home in a wagon, feet foremost, if the Sheriff holds any forced sale and he bids on any of Earle's stock today."

That was all. He waved his hand in a quick gesture, slapped his horse on the rump, and the men fell in behind him. Up through the steep hills, heavy with mid-summer foliage, they followed the narrow, washed-out road.

Walter had never seen nor heard of Moses Earle, but there was no mistaking the Earle place when they reached it. The little house was high on the westerly slope of Dingle Hill, overlooking the green Tremperskill valley. A rail fence enclosed the barnyard and separated Earle's land from the road. In the yard and in the cluster of maple and birch trees beyond, masked horsemen moved restlessly, watching two men—representatives of Landowner Charlotte Verplanck, Walter decided. On the porch of the small frame house an old man sat and rocked.

The leader in red left his new recruits as soon as he had brought them to the farm and Walter found himself among another group of horsemen whom he did not know. Few said anything. He tried to keep near Gerrit but there was a constant shifting and restless riding about in the yard back of the barn.

Walter began to take stock of the "Indians" who far out-numbered any group he had ever been with before. Next to him a heavily built man was riding a horse more handsome than any of the others and Walter wondered if it could be one of the Morgan horses he had heard about. It was a light chestnut with dark flowing mane and tail, broad quarters, a compact back and sinewed legs. The animal carried itself gracefully, with a lofty, elegant action unlike the stubby, squatty farm horses that filled the yard. Except for one white foot its coloring was beautifully uniform.

Walter edged nearer Gerrit and with a nod indicated the chestnut. "There are more than poor tenant farmers here today," he said in a low voice. "That animal didn't come from behind some farmer's plow. I wonder . . ."

He was interrupted by a sudden general movement toward the highway where two men had joined the sheriff and land agent. One was a large fellow with red hair and a growth of ruddy stubble on cheeks and chin, and his name was muttered by more than one "Indian."

"Osman Steele!"

"That's Steele."

"Two years ago he was indicted for assault and beating a women, but he's never been punished."

The "Indians" were crowding nearer to the pasture where Moses Earle's animals stood stolidly in the August sun, swishing their tails at the flies.

Walter following the horse he so admired, took stock of the rider too. His disguise was less flamboyant than the bright calico wrappers around him and for a fleeting instant Walter seemed to remember something like it, then a shout went up and the whole body of masked men formed a hollow square around the four representatives of the law and Moses Earle's animals.

"We're driving the cattle into the highway," Steele shouted. "You stinking outlaws can't stop a sheriff's sale!"

He was answered by derisive whoops.

"You may have mixed gunpowder with your brandy, Steele, but there'll be no sale!"

"Earle's cattle stay in the pasture where they are!"

"We're driving them into the highway," Steele shouted back and began waving his pistol into the air. At least one of the others cooped within the man-made square drew a gun.

Walter was too far back to know who fired first, but he thought it was the sheriff or Steele. More shots rang out, and wild shouting and cursing increased.

"Shoot back! Shoot the horses down!" someone from the "Indian" ranks shouted and the man on the chestnut horse picked up the cry. "Shoot their horses!" His voice rang clearly above the bedlam and more shots were fired. Walter saw one "Indian" fall over his horse's side and a companion hurried to the rescue. At almost the same instant Steele's horse reared and shrieked in agony, then Steele fell from the wounded animal and lay motionless on the ground. Another shot from the "Indians" felled the horse of one of Steele's companions.

Sheriff Moore rushed toward the "Indians," his hands in the air.

"Stop it! Stop it! You may have killed him. Stop before any more men are hurt or killed!"

Osman Steele did not get up.

"If there's a doctor in this crowd, let him come forth," the sheriff pleaded, turning from the masked men to a little crowd of spectators in the road beyond the fence.

One of the men with Steele sent bullets through the heads of the two wounded horses and ended their agonized threshing, and the barnyard was suddenly quiet. Osman Steele was being carried into Moses Earle's little house and from the unmasked spectators a man emerged. His name was whispered from rider to rider. "Dr. John Calhoun of Andres."

"Steele must be hurt bad."

"He isn't moving."

The masked men withdrew from the pasture and barnyard. Walter found Gerrit and kept close to his side. He hadn't expected anything so serious as this to happen when he started that morning to fight for the Delaware farmers. Neither had anyone else, he felt certain. Steele himself had started the shooting, or one of his companions. Whoever fired back must have been maddened by the shrill voice that cried "Shoot back! Shoot them down!"

By late afternoon the red-garbed leader had found one boy among the raiders who was too young and small to be suspected as one of them. Walter watched while the youngster was unmasked and sent circling around the barn and up to the house. He was back in a few minutes and his message passed from man to man: "Steele's shot through in three places and can't live. The chief says to split and squander."

The reaction was instantaneous.

"Get out of Delaware County, Walt," Gerrit ordered. "Get home as fast as you can. There'll be posses on all roads before morning."

"Burn your disguises," someone shouted.

Gerrit started from the county in one direction and Walter in another and Walter found himself trailing the chestnut horse down through the hills, the fleeter animal keeping ahead of Walter and those behind him. Suddenly, from the ravine below, Walter heard other horses' hooves pounding. Reinforcements coming to back up Steele, he imagined. Officers of the law who would challenge them, even if the seriousness of events at Earle's farm were not fully known yet.

Ahead the dark-clad rider was standing in his stirrups tearing off his disguise while the horse raced on. The breeze caught the dress and sent it swirling through the air and into low-hanging branches in front of Walter's eyes. He caught it, jerking it out of his face just in time to see the rider turn the agile chestnut from the road. In one graceful leap, the white forefoot flashing in the air, the animal was across the deep gulley and safely out of sight in the dense undergrowth on the other side.

Walter appraised the rocky crevice. Beyond it lay a jungle of trees and heavy brush where all the horsemen in the raiding party could be hidden while the on-coming posse raced past. But Walter knew his horse could not make that leap, nor could any farm horse. It would be suicidal to attempt it.

Turning his horse around Walter started back, signalling to all he met that a posse was coming up from the valley. Fear deepened the lines on every weather-beaten face as one by one the farmers turned from the road to seek protection in the tree-covered hills.

Walter had a good sense of direction but these winding valleys and steep inclines were strange to him. Better to follow the road until he reached the edge of the wooded section, where he could keep an eye on the cleared fields and pastures while he made his way across country to the Harrison farm. Now was no time to get lost. He must find his way home to-night. By morning every road leading into Delaware County would be guarded. A man hunt would be on for the killers of Osman Steele.

Chapter 10

       Walter did not reach the Harrison farm that night. Keeping within the protecting shadows of the woods took him miles out of his way. To make matters worse, his horse developed a limp at about sunset and in the fading light Walter could not tell whether a stone had lodged under a loose horseshoe or what had happened. He dismounted and progressed even more slowly, letting the animal favor the injured foot.

       Darkness found Walter at the crossroads where the raiders had met the Delaware leader that morning, and he decided it was safer to stay there, close to the great overhanging boulder, than to risk going farther and perhaps getting lost in the woods. He was hungry, and when the moon came up he foraged for wild berries, but the weird midnight noises did not encourage exploration. Deer and moose came crashing down from the hills for water, a cougar's victim shrieked in death agony, and owls kept up their spine-chilling calls. Walter did not try to sleep. He pressed his back against the cold stone and waited for morning.

It was a night for reflection and his thoughts were somber recriminations. Why had he, who had been privileged to hear of the Berne discussions first hand, participate in this "Indian" raid? The Delaware farmers and their reinforcements had not shown themselves responsible today when they answered the shots Steele sent into the air, and the cry of "Shoot them down," with gunfire. Even the injustice of taking all of Moses Earle's stock in payment of a small debt did not warrant the violence he had participated in. Charles Stanton, for all his coldness, was right. Justice could only come through law. Walter buried his face in his hands. Why hadn't he been quick-witted enough to find an honorable way to let Mr. Stanton know the true situation, when he had the opportunity? Now here he was, hiding like an outlaw.

At the first streak of daylight he led his horse from the hollow and into the woods, looking again for wild fruit while he slowly made his way through back fields and wood-lots toward the Harrison home. He misjudged the distance and came upon it from the sugarbush at the back of the farm at about noon. With the thought of a good meal uppermost in mind he hurried the last weary stretch to the house.

Walter unsaddled his horse in the deserted barnyard and rolled the two disguises he still carried into a bundle. He had not dared leave them in the woods; now he could dispose of them in the kitchen fireplace. He was almost at the door when the rhythmic pounding of hooves drew his eyes to the road. A posse was approaching and behind them in a wagon four or five men in homespun rode, guarded by an armed officer.

Walter's feet turned to stone. Only the low-hanging orchard branches protected him from full view until the house was between him and the galloping horses. In a flash of memory he saw Tom Yates clambering into a scrub pine to hide the early "Indian" disguises back home. He reached for the branches of a maple, climbed high into the tree, and was able to grasp the entwining branch of a towering elm beside it. Here in the heavy foliage he and his telltale bundle might escape notice—if he could control his anguished gasps as he pulled himself up to the only possible safety.

Four men raced into the yard and moved with precision, one to the front door, one to the back and two to barns and outbuildings. There were no shouts nor commands. Walter saw Lucretia open the kitchen door, saw her expression change to fear while she stepped aside to let the men enter. Sweat dripped from Walter's forehead and neck and he clung to the limb with arms and legs almost paralyzed with terror.

In minutes the search was over. Mr. Harrison and Gerrit were marched out of the house and the door closed firmly upon the women within. The deputies who had searched the barns returned.

"No one's hiding out there," one man told the officer in charge. "I rammed my bayonet through every pile of straw."

For a few minutes all stood under the tree that sheltered Walter while the deputies scanned the orchard and garden and fields beyond.

"I don't believe the old fellow could get on a horse," the leader said appraising Mr. Harrison's bent figure. "The table wasn't set for more, so likely they're telling the truth and two men are all there is."

"We'll take the young one in then," another proposed. "Let the old one stay."

They marched Mr. Harrison back to the kitchen door and once more Walter saw it firmly closed. What was happening inside?

Gerrit did not protest when a gun barrel pointed to the road. He walked silently to the wagon and joined the prisoners there.

113

Walter waited until the armed men and dejected farmers were out of sight before he slid to the ground. His heart was pounding and his voice unsteady when he opened the kitchen door.

"Susan! Lucretia! Don't be frightened."

"Walter!" Susan gasped. She was holding Lucretia's head against her shoulder, helping her toward a chair. Elias toddled from them to grab at one of Walter's legs, his round eyes staring from one silent person to another in bewilderment.

"They've just taken Gerrit," Mr. Harrison said hoarsely.

"I know," Walter told them. "I was up in the elm tree. Did they say anything? What are they going to do?"

"They're asking the governor to declare martial law in Delaware County," Susan said. "The sheriff has called for volunteers to swell the ranks of his deputies. Those who took Gerrit were civil enough. I guess it's their duty to maintain law and order."

"But for how long? How long . . . ?" Walter stopped before the anguished look on Lucretia's face. No one knew how long Gerrit would be imprisoned, and it was plain that Mr. Harrison feared the worst when he spoke.

"The Schoharie County officers got wind of our intention to help the Delaware 'Indians' and they've been rounding up farmers here," he told Walter. "They're holding the ones they get in the Brimstone church and the jail at Gilboa. Since I've been so active in the anti-rent movement, they've been here twice. Gerrit would have been taken in by that gang yesterday if they'd found him here. These deputies were from Delaware County."

The old man extended a twisted hand for Elias and stroked the baby's head gently when he came.

"Walt, the road here is safe, now that they've just covered it and rounded up all the men they could find," he went on. "There may be more searching parties along tomorrow, or even tonight, hunting again for those who hid out in caves and woods. Go home now, while you can, and let your folks know what's happened. Ask your Pa if he can spare you to take in the crops for Gerrit and me. If the grain isn't harvested now everything will be lost and we'll have nothing—either of us."

Even Susan paled at his words. Walter nodded numbly and held out his bundle. "Better burn this," he suggested, handing it to Susan.

She unrolled the calico and came to the second disguise and her expression changed to surprise.

"What's this? Where did you get it?"

Walter told her of the "Indian" on the chestnut horse and of the leap that took the fortunate rider to safety.

Susan tossed Walter's cheap wrapper into the fire but she held the flowered black goods in her hands, examining the design of the dress and workmanship.

"This is no farm wife's Mother Hubbard," she said. "It wasn't made for the one who wore it, either. See where the sleeves are torn from the back so the man could get into it?"

She turned it around once more. "French seams sewn with linen thread. Fine buttonholes. I'd like to see the one who wore this."

"So would I," Walter agreed. "If there really were rich and influential men riding with us yesterday, he was one. And he was the one whose frenzy started the men shooting."

"Hide it somewhere, Susan," Mr. Harrison suggested. "They aren't likely to search here again. If Walt ever sees the horse he might trace the rider. It might be someone who could help us. Now, Walt, get started home before anything else happens."

Walter looked at the table hungrily and hesitated. Sensing his need, Susan dropped the disguise on an empty chair.

"He's starved," she said. "When did you eat last? Here,

sit down and I'll warm up the gravy. Lucretia, you didn't finish feeding Elias, either."

The busyness of warming the food and making fresh tea restored something of normalcy to the Harrison household. Elias and Walter were hungry, and although Susan could not pretend cheerfulness she ate with them, prodding her sister and the Harrisons to try a few bites. She walked with Walter to the barn when they had finished and together they looked at the horse's hoof.

"I think it's a sharp stone or root under the shoe," Walter said. "I can't see anything though, can you?"

She peered at the foot Walter held in his hands. "The leg isn't swollen," she observed. "Is your blacksmith a good veterinarian?"

"Yes. He'll know what's wrong."

He put the foot down and for a few moments they stood beside the horse, stroking the gentle bay's shoulder. Susan wasn't as tall as Walter. Her waving curls were at his eye level.

"Walter . . . ?" For the first time she sounded unsure of herself.

"Yes, Susan."

"Will your Pa let you come back? I don't think Gerrit will be home soon."

"Pa'll let me come. He has John," Walter reassured her. "But what makes you say that?"

"I talked with the man who came to the front door while the rest were in the kitchen," she explained. "He told me Osman Steele died of his wounds. And they've got Dr. Boughton imprisoned for a second trial. This time they mean business. He said . . ."

She looked away from him and her fingers closed tightly over the horse's coarse mane.

"He said if anyone identifies Gerrit it will go bad with

him. It'll mean jail. That's where he's being taken now. To Delhi, to jail."

She whispered the word and involuntarily Walter shuddered. Gerrit had been identified once before and in the darkness of a winter night, too. There had been spectators watching in the road in front of Moses Earle's house that afternoon—men from whose ranks the physician had come. No one had paid much attention to them but now Walter wondered who they were and where they had come from.

"Don't worry, Susan," he said trying to keep his voice steady. "It's Delaware County that's involved. Maybe they'll let him go when they find out he's from Schoharie."

He didn't believe it himself and he was sure Susan doubted it.

"Do you really think your Pa'll let you come back?" she repeated. "I don't know how I can manage without you."

The blue eyes were dark with anxiety. It was Susan whose shoulders would have to take the burden of Gerrit's family now unless he shared it. Work in the garden storing food for winter. Work in the fields, if any harvesting was done. If Lucretia didn't make herself sick and take to her bed, it would be a mercy.

"Pa'll let me come. I'll be back as soon as I can."

She stood in the barnyard, hands clasped in front of her, and watched him go. From the road he turned for a last look at her—gold curls and a brave red ribbon.

The trip to town in the August heat was slow, for Walter could not hurry his weary horse. Mind and body were tired when at last he reached the familiar street, and he wondered dully at the unusual number of people riding up and down. There were farmers at the blacksmith shop too, but none he knew well and he had no desire to get into a conversation with them. The story he had to tell was for Pa alone. He sat

117

on a stump beside the building, away from the glowing forge in front, disregarding the unusual commotion around him.

Suddenly a bugle call sounded above the ringing blows of the blacksmith's hammer. Startled, Walter got to his feet and for a second stood beside the wall of the building hoping no one would see him. These men couldn't be looking for him, miles away from the Delaware misadventure, he assured himself and walked to the street. Two horsemen halted in front of the forge and behind them Peter Ten Nuys sat straight-backed on his mount, the gun across his saddle reflecting the glint of the setting sun.

"By the authority of the sheriff of Delaware County I call for volunteers!" The man with the bugle shouted his message twice.

The half a dozen riders straggled around Peter stiffened in their saddles and affected a military bearing. Beyond them youngsters stared and small dogs yapped.

The blacksmith turned his back to the street and struck a resounding, defiant blow, drawing all eyes to his glowing forge. The farm men shifted uncomfortably while they waited for their animals to be shod.

Walter knew he would be challenged the instant Peter saw him, and remembering Peter's discomfiture at his hands in Berne, he could scarcely expect anything except a miserable time of it. He took a long breath and waited while Peter rode from the group in the street to the cinder patch in front of the forge.

"Well, Walter, you heard the call to duty," Peter said. "You know of the insurrection in Delaware County? Or hasn't the word reached your back clearings?"

"I know," Walter replied, smarting at the tone and the belittling reference to the farms but determined to keep his head.

"The Berne convention pledged to abide by law and maintain order," Peter reminded him. "Aren't you with your own leaders?"

"Berne was right. I stand where I stood then," Walter replied.

"Now is your chance to prove it!" Peter squared his shoulders. On his horse he towered above Walter and the farmers at the forge. "We're calling for volunteers to round up the outlaws who defied the law and killed Osman Steele."

The deputies and their recruits were riding nearer and the blacksmith and his customers were silent, watching Walter and waiting for his reply.

There was only one answer. Walter was surprised at the evenness of his voice when he spoke.

"I can never turn against the farmers anywhere, even if they're misguided in what they do. We will stand by each other as long as life lasts."

Unconsciously Walter had repeated the words of the old "Indian" oath, and although Peter did not recognize them the men at the forge did. Shoulders squared and backs straightened with a defiance they had not dared to show before, and the blacksmith called to Walter by name.

"Platt, bring up your horse. You're next."

Walter wasn't sure it was his turn, but he had spoken for these men from the back roads and they were with him. They watched while the blacksmith cared for his horse, applying medicine to the injured foot and replacing the worn shoe. Then they clapped him on the shoulder when he faced into the fading red and amber night and rode away.

If only he could speak for them where his words would count! If only he, not Peter Ten Nuys, had been given that recommendation from Pastor Camp!

Walter had been away from home less than a week, but

119

there was a strangeness about the kitchen when he entered it. His parents were working at odd chores, and in the flickering candlelight he saw the silver sheen in his mother's hair, the deepened lines in his father's face.

"Walt!" Relief sounded in his father's voice.

"We'd begun to worry a little," Ma said, questioning him with her look.

"What do you know about the Delaware uprising?" Pa asked keeping his voice even.

To tell them was the hardest thing Walter had ever done. They listened, and didn't interrupt. Their faces, hardened by sun and wind, toil and heartaches, were masks that hid their emotions. One more blow, Walter thought, and he the one who must tell them.

"To Delhi," Pa repeated when Walter finished. "They took all the men to Delhi?"

"That's what Susan was told."

For a few minutes the ticking clock was the only sound in the kitchen.

"I wonder if we can see him," Pa said at last. "We'll have to find out what to do. I wish we knew more about what the law is, and how to get a fair trial for Gerrit."

That was all. No word of blame, no questioning of his sons' bad judgment. Walter wondered if Pa was thinking of Charles Stanton but the name wasn't mentioned nor was Pastor Camp's, although they were the only ones Walter knew who might tell them what to do—unless it was the "Indian" on the chestnut horse.

"Is there anything you need for the harvesting?" Pa asked. "Has Mr. Harrison all the tools? Everything you'll need?"

"I'm sure he has," Walter answered. "Can you manage with John?"

"What else?" Pa asked. He got up slowly and walked to

120

the open door where the night breeze brought relief from the heat. "This Susan. What is she like?"

"She's strong. Healthy and strong and not like Lucretia," Walter told his father. "She isn't big but she can help me with the grain. Old Mr. Harrison can get the vegetables in, and we'll manage. They may free the farmers from outside Delaware, too, Pa."

"Pray God," Ma whispered.

"Yes, pray God," Pa said and sighed. "Now watch your horse and take care of it between now and Sunday. When we go to church maybe we can find out what to do."

"If Peter comes home from Delaware between now and then he'll tell his father what's happening there," Walter agreed. "For once I'm glad Derick Ten Nuys and Pastor Camp are friends, for this way Pastor Camp will know."

From some source Pastor Camp had late news from Delaware—news that was far from encouraging.

"You musn't try to go," he told Pa. "Posses are out on every road, rounding up farmers and not using any judgment. The reports are frightening. I'll go with Walter tomorrow. A minister of the gospel is safe. For once it's an asset not to be built like Gerrit, Walter. You don't look any more than your seventeen years."

They rode in the minister's carriage, Walter's horse tied behind. With Lucretia in mind Walter urged Pastor Camp to go first to the Harrison farm and when it came in sight he pointed out the acres of ripening grain, the loaded fruit trees and the sugarbush beyond.

"This is a bad time for Gerrit to be away," he said thinking of the work that had to be done now, and the rest of the year.

Pastor Camp let the reins drop loose and turned from his contemplation of the horses' swaying flanks to look at Walter.

"What is it going to mean to you, Walter, if this time Gerrit doesn't get out scot-free?" he asked. "Suppose the talk is right, and the men they're holding in Delhi get jail sentences."

Walter looked into the penetrating blue eyes, shuddering at the suggestion and uncertain how to answer.

"I don't know," he finally said. "I haven't even thought. I've just got to do what has to be done, day by day now."

Pastor Camp lay a kindly hand on Walter's knee. "That's all you can do now, I guess. We are 'our brother's keeper.' "

"And our sister's too," Walter said leaning forward in the seat. "Something must have happened."

In the barnyard Susan was hitching the horses to the old farm wagon, too intent upon her task to notice their arrival. As soon as the carriage slowed to a halt Walter was out, running toward her.

"What are you doing?" he called. "Where are you going?"

At the sound of his voice Lucretia came from the house, carrying baskets in either hand, Mr. Harrison hobbling out behind her.

"Lucretia! Susan! What are you doing?" Walter repeated.

"I'm going to Gerrit!" Lucretia hurried past him toward the wagon. "How do I know whether he has decent food? Or a blanket to lie upon?"

"Wait a minute," Pastor Camp warned. "I'm not sure it's safe for you to go."

"That's what I've told her," Mr. Harrison agreed. "She won't listen to me, though. Nor can Susan reason with her."

"Let them throw me in jail with him," Lucretia sobbed, going past them. "No one can stop me."

Wrestling with the tug of a harness Susan looked at Walter, shook her head and looked away. It was clear to them all that Lucretia was determined.

"We'll go with you then," Pastor Camp said calmly. "They won't throw a woman in jail but we may be turned back. Walter, put up our horses."

Only a few braved the roads leading into Delaware County that day. Twice on the trip to Delhi Walter saw posses riding through farmers' grain fields, overturning shocks where men might be hiding, their horses stamping on the grain. Fields where harvesters should have been working were deserted. When they neared the town Walter could hear axe blows and hammers ringing, and see a crowd of men working near the town meeting house.

"What are they doing?" Susan asked, clutching at one of the baskets. At the sight of the crowd she appeared more alarmed than Lucretia.

"Building an addition to the jail is my guess," Pastor Camp said. "If they've really rounded up more than a hundred men, the old jail won't hold them all."

He was right. A stockade of logs had been put up behind the two story meeting house and inside it barracks were being erected. The yard was filled with men hauling lumber or at work with saws and hammers, and possemen on horseback galloped up and down the street, guns and bayonets glistening. Delhi was like a city at war.

Walter drew the horses to a halt a little distance from the meeting house, uncertain whether they should move closer. The moment they stopped Lucretia had a foot on the wagon wheel and was out, one basket in her hand.

"I'll have to go with her," Susan said. "Heaven knows what she'll do."

Walter turned to Pastor Camp in dismay. The girls were both running across the open yard toward the mounted men patrolling the newly built stockade.

"I can't let them go alone," he said and handed the reins to the minister.

Dashing after the girls Walter looked ahead to the men on guard and almost stopped in surprise. Side by side with an older man in uniform was Peter Ten Nuys, curiously watching Lucretia and Susan while the other man tried to wave them back. But Lucretia went on and desperately Walter followed.

"I've met you somewhere I know," Walter heard Peter saying to Lucretia when she reached him. Then he looked at Susan appraisingly and slid from his horse. "I haven't ever seen you though. I wish we were meeting under different circumstances."

He reached for the basket Susan carried. "I'd like to help you," he said with a show of gallantry just as Walter reached the girls. Annoyed, he turned his back on Walter and once more directed his attention to Susan. "Who did you want to see?"

"Gerrit Platt, my husband," Lucretia broke in eagerly, moving closer to him an appeal on her strained face.

"Gerrit Platt!" Peter looked at Lucretia again and pushed Susan's basket back toward her. "I should have remembered you, of course."

The stern-faced officer rode nearer.

"Do you know this Gerrit Platt?" he asked Peter. "Can you identify him?"

Peter had a foot in the stirrup and was mounting his horse again. "I can identify him as one of an 'Indian' band that burned the Van Rensselaer building back home, and I will," Peter said, the smile he had given Susan vanishing.

"Identify him . . . ?" Susan whispered the horrifying words and turned to Walter, fear draining the color from her face.

Chapter **11**

Osman Steele was shot and killed on August 7, 1845 and twenty days later Walter learned that Governor Wright had declared martial law in Delaware County. The raids of the sheriff and his volunteer posses were terrorizing the countryside, doing more damage than any activities carried out by the disguised farmers. Two hundred men were said to be behind the Delhi stockade, and armed mobs were looking for more. Farmers hid in caves, under hastily built false floors in hay mows or granaries, and in the remote ravines of the Catskill foothills. Women took food to them at night, did what they could about the harvest rotting in the fields, and lived in fear.

Late in September Pa came unexpectedly to the Harrison farm. Without stopping at the house he hurried to the field where Walter and Susan, with Mr. Harrison's feeble help, were finishing their day's work in the fading purple sunset. They saw him coming and waited, not knowing whether to be glad or apprehensive.

"We've got to get a lawyer for Gerrit now," Pa told them as soon as the introductions were over. "Gerrit hasn't been released nor has anyone else. I don't know what it will cost, but if it takes all I've got we must do it."

The urgency in Pa's tone alarmed Walter. "Have you heard anything about the trials?" he asked. "It's been almost two months and no date set, according to the last papers I saw."

Pa hesitated, looked at Susan and Mr. Harrison, and apparently decided he could trust them with the news.

"Big Thunder's second trial has just ended," he said. "The jury found him guilty of robbery, but they say John Van Buren had more influence with Judge Edmonds than the jury, and forced a different decision." He paused before telling how the case ended. "Judge Edmonds said he was guilty of high treason and sentenced him to life in Clinton prison at Dannemora."

"Life?" Walter gasped the word and it was echoed by Susan and Mr. Harrison.

"Now they say 'Handsome John' is on his way to Delhi. He'll prosecute there for the state too, as attorney general," Pa finished.

For a moment they stood, speechless in the stubble.

"A share of the harvest belongs to Gerrit, of course." Mr. Harrison's voice was shaking. "Get the best lawyer you can."

Walking back to the house, Walter and Susan told Pa of their fearsome knowledge of Peter's intentions. It was the first time they had let Mr. Harrison know.

"But Peter can't identify Gerrit as one of the men at Moses Earle's place," Pa exclaimed. "We know, and bitterly do I regret it, but unless someone identifies Gerrit as one of the Delaware 'Indians' how can he be convicted?"

It was their one hope, but Walter took little comfort from it. The rumors spreading among the farm people gave little encouragement that those under arrest would be freed.

"We musn't let Gerrit know Peter's going to take the stand against him," Walter cautioned. "Tell the attorney, but not Gerrit. Things must look bad enough for him without that worry. What can we say to encourage him, if we're allowed to see him at all?"

"Tell him the harvest's almost all done," Susan spoke up, then involuntarily hid her scratched and blistered hands behind her back. Working in the fields from the first light of dawn until night drove them in, pulling potatoes and root vegetables from the garden patch by moonlight, Walter and Susan and Mr. Harrison had saved most of the crops.

"It's fortunate Walter has you," Pa said and both he and Walter looked at her in silent thankfulness. In her faded calico wrapper, sunbonnet falling off the back of her head, curls tied with a wisp of sumac-dyed yarn, she was a staunch little figure, assurance and determination in every line of her face and every gesture.

"We've all worked," Susan told Pa, seeming to sense his feeling about Lucretia. "Lou's brought hot food to us in the fields three times a day so we didn't waste time going to the house. And she's done all the work there, now that Mrs. Harrison can't get out of her chair."

"I'm glad you've all kept well," Pa said gently. "We've got a lot to tell Gerrit to be thankful for. Lucretia'll be glad we're trying to see him again, but I don't think you girls should come with Walt and me tomorrow."

Lucretia had seen Pa go into the fields without stopping at the house and she extended a hand to him uncertainly when they went into the kitchen. To Walter's surprise he put his arm around her shoulder and bending down, kissed her on the forehead. It was the comfort she needed. Her arms reached up around his neck and tears filled her eyes.

"Don't be ashamed to cry," Pa said. "Tomorrow Walt

127

and I are going to Delhi and if it's safe for you and Susan to come, one of us will be back for you. We're going to get a lawyer for Gerrit."

She accepted Pa's decision without protest. With him at the supper table that night they all felt a new safety.

Pa was not the only one who had heard that John Van Buren, flushed with victory, would prosecute the Delhi prisoners. Wagons and oxcarts, like dark red beetles, crawled around the curves and over the hills ahead of them, and into the little town. Its streets were patrolled by uniformed and armed militia. The jail had been completed in the weeks since Walter was there, and its white facade presented a neat appearance. Hitching their horses a distance away, Walter and Pa started for the building, keeping out of the way of galloping horsemen and avoiding their hostile looks.

It was the changing of the guard, they soon realized. Mounted men at the front and rear of the stockade snapped salutes at each other, and with consternation Walter once more recognized Peter as one of those taking up the post at the gate where they had last seen each other.

"Pa! We can't ask anything of Peter!" Walter stopped where he stood, staring at the two men on horseback who now had command of the entrance. "He wasn't even civil to Lucretia and Susan when we were here before."

Pa looked up and down the street, then back to the prison gate. Peter had seen them, said something to the man with him, and now both were watching silently.

"Come on," Pa said. "For Gerrit's sake we'll have to try. I'll do the talking."

It didn't seem to Walter that he could once more walk to that stockade and ask Peter Ten Nuys anything. But for Gerrit—Gerrit who had been behind those walls almost two months now—they had to.

"Good day, Peter," he heard his father saying. "Is a parent allowed to see his son inside?"

Peter did not return the greeting. "I have no authority to permit it," he replied brusquely, looking at Pa and ignoring Walter. Pa turned to the other guard.

"Have you the authority?" he asked.

"I have not," was the answer. "We're guards."

"To keep prisoners inside and all others outside," Peter amplified. He looked over Pa's head, chin set and shoulders stiff in the military manner.

"Who has, then?" Pa persisted.

When neither guard answered, a small boy who had been observing the encounter spoke up. "If you've got a son inside, you'd best see Amasa Parker or Samuel Gordon," he advised with a great show of importance. "They're attorneys for the prisoners."

"Thank you," Pa said to the boy. "I thought Amasa Parker was the judge."

"There's two of 'em," the boy told him as he and Walter started away. "The old one's the attorney and his nephew's the judge. A grand jury's hearing cases every day now. You'll find all three of 'em in the meeting house."

Walter and Pa walked to the front of the building and following their ears, found themselves at the entrance to the jury room. Seated at one side were the jury members, and at a glance Walter's heart fell. There certainly wasn't a farmer among them. Well-dressed, prosperous appearing men, picked from the towns beyond a doubt, they looked at the bedraggled, unshaven youth whose testimony was being taken with unconcealed contempt.

The language of the man who was questioning the prisoner was profane and shocking to Walter. When the frightened man insisted he had not been at the Moses Earle farm on the day Osman Steele was shot, he was cursed for a liar and a fool, and told he would fare better if he pleaded guilty.

Pa and Walter waited until the ordeal was over, then Pa inquired which lawyer was Samuel Gordon.

"The judge's uncle isn't the man to be defending the farmers," he said in an aside to Walter. "The landowners pick the judges. Everyone knows that."

Samuel Gordon shook his head when Pa told his errand. "You haven't come too soon," the lawyer said. "If I recall correctly, Platt's to be questioned tomorrow. Little time to prepare a case for him, but I'll do what I can."

Walter listened while his father said what he could on Gerrit's behalf—that he was a resident of Schoharie county not Delaware, and that he had not belonged to the anti-rent associations in either of those counties.

"I'll not be given much time," Mr. Gordon warned Pa. "We've been told the hearings are to be finished in three weeks, then the men will all be sentenced on one day and have it over."

"All sentenced on one day?" Walter broke in. "Is it all settled in advance that they're all guilty? Before the hearings, even?"

The lawyer looked at him as though he were a child who had spoken out of turn and didn't answer except to repeat that he'd do what he could. Then he turned and left them, saying he'd talk to Gerrit.

"What he can do isn't going to be much, Pa," Walter said when they were alone.

Pa started down the steps and toward the wagon where they would spend the night, to save the price of a room at the inn.

"We should have another lawyer," he told Walter. "I didn't know the hearings were being rushed through like this.

Parker's as good as a prosecutor, not one to defend the men. I didn't tell you, but the foreman of the grand jury is a relative of one of the sheriff's chief deputies."

Worse news than that waited them the next day when they returned to the juryroom. Seated opposite the jurors were the officers and deputies who were taking testimony against the prisoners and among them was Peter Ten Nuys. He was talking seriously with a well-dressed and exceedingly handsome young man and did not look in the direction of the prisoner's box or the spectators who were crowding into the room. John Van Buren, Walter guessed, had come. It was yesterday's prosecutor who stood beside him, talking to Peter.

Pa pushed Walter in ahead of him. "Get near where they had that poor devil sitting yesterday," he whispered. "That's where Gerrit'll be today. Gordon will have told him we're here and he'll be looking for us. We may even be able to talk to him."

The noise in the room grew more intense while the jurors waited for the officers to bring in each new prisoner. One pleaded guilty to manslaughter, another to unlawful assemblage, then Gerrit was ushered into the room, militiamen holding him by either arm. Somehow he had managed to get shaved, and although his clothes were wrinkled they were clean. His hair needed cutting, but he had slicked it back in long waves from his forehead.

Gerrit Platt was still undefeated. He stood erect, half a head taller than the men who guarded him, his shoulders straight and his step firm. His eyes at once searched the spectators and when they found Pa and Walter, gratitude shown above the concern he must have felt for himself.

Short work was made of the preliminaries. The prosecutor was ready for this case and Peter was sworn in as a witness immediately. Hand on the Bible he promised to tell the truth.

"Can you identify the prisoner?" the prosecutor asked, while Van Buren fixed a searching look upon him.

"I can." There was no uncertainty or hesitation. "I know him to be Gerrit Platt."

"Tell the jurors what you know of him," Peter was instructed.

"I know him to be a member of an anti-rent band of 'Indians.' I've seen him in his disguise." He looked balefully at Gerrit. "They burned the land office in Rensselaerwyck."

"That's enough!" the prosecutor thundered. "I remind you that in 1839 Governor Seward warned that insurrection is treason, punishable by death. Can anyone say it was not insurrection that took place on Moses Earle's farm? I demand that this man be charged with murder."

Murder! The word stunned Walter, but Pa must have been prepared. He pushed his way to Mr. Gordon. Across the room Walter saw Peter pale at the charge and look from the jurors to the stunned spectators until at last he saw Walter. He started to sit down, thought better of it, and remained standing but he couldn't meet Walter's blazing eyes. Around the prisoner's box there was confusion while Mr. Gordon questioned Gerrit, talked to Pa, conferred with the others and finally got the attention of the judge. The testimony, he pointed out, had not identified Gerrit as one of the Delaware "Indians" nor as present at the Moses Earle farm. The prisoner would not plead guilty to murder but he would to a lesser charge, if the court would permit.

So Gerrit pleaded guilty to unlawful assemblage in disguise.

They followed him out of the courthouse, Walter and Pa, into the funereal silence of the yard. For a few minutes they were allowed to talk to him, Pa gripping his hand all the time.

132

"We'll not desert you, son," Pa told him. "I should have acted sooner. We should have had another lawyer. One from outside this county."

"I doubt if any lawyer could have done anything after Peter's testimony," Gerrit said. "There's no justice in courts controlled by the landowners. Not for the farmers. There are smart and educated men in this jail and they all say the same thing. That jury isn't listening to anything but what they want to hear. It's the same thing each time a man comes back from the hearings. Moses Earle never left his porch that day, but they're going to find him guilty of murder."

"There'll be a way to get a new trial, or maybe a pardon," Pa insisted. We'll find out what to do. Just know that we'll not desert you nor give up."

For a few seconds they were allowed to stand together, and Gerrit put an arm around Walter's shoulder.

"Lucretia? Elias?" he asked, his voice hoarse when he spoke their names.

"They're fine," Walter assured him.

"We'll take care of them," Pa promised. "If I can find out when the sentencing is I'll bring them so you can see them at least, if the worst happens."

Then the guards took Gerrit away, back through the white front of the Delhi jail.

Two weeks later Pa came once more to the Harrison farm. The sentence was to be October 11, and he tried to prepare Lucretia for it.

"Pretty yourself up, girl," he said. "It maybe the last look Gerrit has at you and the baby for months. Don't let it be a glum picture."

So Susan and Lucretia both dressed in their silk dresses, with white ruching at the neck, and with their best bonnets setting off their curls, but no one tried to smile. They drove to Delhi under an overcast sky, bronzed and yellowed leaves whipped along the road ahead of them by a chill breeze. There was no ray of sunshine and the heavens above were ready to weep for Gerrit Platt and the other Delhi prisoners.

"Susan, you'd better stay outside with the baby," Pa suggested. "If he should fuss we might all get ordered out. Lucretia can sit between Walter and me."

He had planned it well, and had warned Lucretia she would hear men sentenced to jail, but the bare walls, the hard benches, the rough tables and the stern-faced men were frightening.

More so were the first sentences. Two men who had refused to plead guilty to any charge were summoned first. In quick succession they were sentenced to be hanged.

Gasps of astonishment, quickened breathing, and a hush in the room. That was all. Walter couldn't believe he was hearing right. Beside him Lucretia shuddered and Pa's arm went across the back of the bench, his hand resting on her shoulder. Walter stared at the glowering judge, meeting out a justice that to him was murderous. Did no one dare to speak out?

Moses Earle was next. An old man, bent and frightened, he pleaded guilty to manslaughter.

"Life imprisonment!" roared Judge Parker.

The weight on Walter's chest was almost pain. Three men were called before this bar of justice and sentenced to prison for life. The room was becoming deathly still except for a voice calling the names of the prisoners, the creaking of floor boards beneath the heavy tread of the officers and their victims, and the merciless words of the judge.

"Gerrit Platt!"

Pa's hand gripped Lucretia's shoulder and Walter braced himself. Once more he watched the brother he had loved all his life, cross the room and stand beside the bare table. Saw the blue eyes searching for his family.

". . . has pleaded guilty to unlawful assemblage. . . ." the prosecutor was intoning.

Judge Parker scarcely waited for the sentence to end.

"Ten years at hard labor in Clinton prison!"

Ten years! Walter couldn't be hearing right. This couldn't be happening. It must be a nightmare.

"Gerrit!" Lucretia was out of Pa's grasp like a wild bird, flying down the aisle toward her husband and crying his name hysterically. "Gerrit! Gerrit!"

She got only a few steps before Pa had her in his arms and carried her, screaming, out of the room while behind them Judge Parker banged on the table and shouted for order.

With feet like lead Walter followed his father, realizing dully that Lucretia's cries had stopped. She was lying limp now in Pa's arms, her head falling off his shoulder, her lips blue and parted. He carried her down the steps to the place where Susan waited. At the sight of them she pushed Elias from her lap to the sere grass beside her and brought the smelling salts from her bag.

"Get water, Walt," she directed. "There's the well and a dipper hanging."

Susan had expected it, he thought. Expected a sentence of more than the months Pa had warned them of. He pumped the water and held the dipper low while Susan bathed Lucretia's head, now cradled against Pa's shoulders. His hands trembled and the dipper tipped, spilling what water was left. Walter got from his knees to return to the pump.

Standing beside them was Peter Ten Nuys.

"You!" It was a groan, coming from Walter's heart. "You! Are you satisfied at last? Have you had your revenge?"

"Walt, I didn't know," Peter's face was pale, his voice

frightened. "I didn't know the sentences would be like that!"

But Walter's mounting fury knew no reason nor mercy. He struck at Peter with the dipper, hitting him heavily on the arm that came up in self-defence.

Peter didn't try to strike back when Walter beat at him. He held his arms before his face and took the blows on back and shoulders while Walter drove him, stumbling, to the courthouse steps.

"Walter, please get the water."

From beyond the storm of his frenzy and desperation Susan's voice came to him. He went to the well.

Chapter *12*

Chip! Chop! Chip!

Once more Walter whittled spiles from sumac branches but he wasn't taking time now to smooth and finish them with his Sheffield knife as he had done last winter at home. His strokes with the old wood carver knife were swift, keeping time with Lucretia's nervous step on the treadle of her spinning wheel. Elias, two years old now, played with the peeled and shining sticks, sniffing in delight at the spice smell of the wood.

It would take at least five times as many spiles for the Harrison sugarbush as Walter had needed to prepare at home. Much of the income from this farm came from the maple sugar and syrup, and half of that income belonged to Gerrit. Some to himself, Walter had been told by Mr. Harrison, only that didn't matter. The Platt share, all Pa had saved, all Susan could earn teaching the common shool would go to engage a lawyer for Gerrit if Governor Wright didn't grant the petitions for pardons.

There was hope that he might, Walter tried to tell himself. When Horace Greeley appealed for commuting the two death sentences imposed at Delhi they had been reduced to life imprisonment, only no one so influential as Horace Greeley had interceded for the others.

Petitions . . . petitions . . . petitions!

What good do they do, Walter had asked his father. Names on pieces of paper. The farmers, begging once more like serfs for justice which never should have been denied them.

"Give the governor a year," Pa had said. "If he doesn't act, perhaps another election will give us another governor. That's Dr. Butler's advice."

Chip! Chop! Chip!

It was getting dark so he must stop and do the barnyard chores while there still was light.

"Lucretia, have you any idea exactly how many spiles Gerrit had to make last year?" Walter asked.

"No, but Mr. Harrison can tell you," she answered. "There are fifty trees to an acre and five or more acres in trees, so you can figure. About one third of them are old trees taking two and three sap buckets."

"It seems to me Mr. Harrison could have helped with this job," Walter muttered, more to himself than to Lucretia.

"Walter, don't you get edgy," Lucretia warned. "He'd only cut himself and I'd have more trouble if it was bad. You'll get them done in time."

"If the sap doesn't start early," Walter acknowledged. "Only how I'm to manage that sugarbush alone, I don't know. One man can't, Lucretia."

Lucretia didn't argue. "It's a good bush," she said. "Gerrit thinned out the young trees and kept the grass and weeds out of the litter of humus. He told me those maples had the best crown he'd seen last summer." She said it proudly. Everything

Gerrit ever had said or done was precious to Lucretia and she talked about him all the time.

Walter put the knife out of Elias' reach and prepared to go to the barn. It was a large sugarbush and well-kept, as Lucretia had said, with a good growth of hemlock and spruce to break the wind and protect the maples. Fencing had kept the animals out. In the saphouse there were at least 500 buckets waiting to be cleaned and tested, besides the 18-quart gathering pails, the huge gathering barrels and the storage tanks for the sap. Everything had to be checked, cleaned and put in order for much of their income depended on it, only how could he and Lucretia and Susan do the work, even if Susan gave up her school to help him? The sap wouldn't wait, once it started running. Empty those buckets or loose the precious juice, that was all there was to it. Then boil all night, skimming, stirring, ten or twelve hours. Pour the sirup into the pound molds and the two-pound molds at just the right time to get a good grade of sugar. He'd be finished with one day's sap in time to do the morning barn chores. Only he didn't think the entire bush could be harvested, even if Susan closed her school, and she'd have to. The sugar crop meant more than the little she was paid for teaching. He hadn't said anything to her about it yet, but he'd have to. Tonight perhaps.

Walter trudged along the path beaten in the snow to the barn. The animals were in good shape and he was grateful for that as he led them to the trough for water. Fresh straw for bedding, grain in the feed bins, then the milking. It all took time and there was so little time for the work that must be done.

Susan came home from school before he had finished, bringing her horse to the barn and caring for it herself as she always did. Her cheerful greeting almost irritated Walter this evening. There was nothing to be cheerful about.

"I've a surprise for you tonight," she called to him. "Something I've been hoping I could lay my hands on for months."

"Yes?" Walter asked trying to be interested. "What is it?"

"You'll see. It's at the house."

He mumbled thanks. Some little thing such as she was always doing, trying to keep the household from sinking into silent despair. He'd thank her properly when the time came. Now he was trying to figure out how they could manage the sugar harvest.

It was still on his mind when he took the milk to the buttery, poured it into the shining pans, and went to the kitchen to wash. Elias ran to him with outstretched arms and baby chatter, and Mr. Harrison looked up from his contemplation of the food the girls were taking to the table to inquire about the weather.

Then Walter saw the book. At his place at the table was a battered copy of "The Revised Statutes of 1821."

"Susan! Where did you get it?" he asked. A law book was the last thing he had expected and he fingered the frayed leather binding hardly believing it could really be there.

Susan brought a steaming bowl of creamed salt codfish to the table, her cheeks flushed from bending over the open fireplace and her eyes bright.

"I've been trying all winter. Ever since I got my first teaching money," she told him. "I asked the parents of all my boys and girls to keep looking, and finally one of them found a cheap copy I could buy."

"You bought it? Not just borrowed it?" It was unbelievable and he carried the treasure to the high mantle where it would be safe, thumbing through the torn pages as he walked across the room. "Susan, I hope you didn't pay too much for it. I've come to the conclusion we've got to try to hire someone to help with the sugar or we're going to lose part of the crop."

Mr. Harrison pushed his chair noisily ahead of him across the kitchen floor to the table. "Walt's right," he said. "You three can't do it alone. I've always had help from the farms with no sugarbushes, or just small ones."

"And we'll have to pay," Walter emphasized. "I can't promise to work in exchange. It'll be all I can do to manage the planting."

His face darkened at the thought. More long, hard hours in the fields next spring and summer, doing work he disliked, but how could he escape it? If he and Lucretia went home to Pa, Mr. Harrison would find someone else to take Gerrit's place—someone who would want to buy the lease, of course. Then Gerrit would have nothing, and no place to go but home again, when he at last was free.

Walter's dark mood permeated the room and the supper hour and even the thought of the law book couldn't change it. As soon as the meal was over he went back to his pile of sumac sticks, whittling more slowly in the uncertain candle light. Lucretia and Susan finished the kitchen work together and when Lucretia took Elias upstairs to bed, Susan sat down on a little three-legged stool beside him instead of going at once to her spinning wheel.

"I thought you'd be more pleased about the book" she said almost wistfully. "It's the basic book for the study of law."

"How can I study law?" The bitterness he felt crept into his voice.

"How can you give it up?" Susan asked. "Walt, we've got to plan. Something beyond the next day's work."

"What do you mean?"

"Gerrit's still in jail. Suppose there isn't any pardon. You talk of getting a lawyer but where is there a lawyer you can rely upon? What did the lawyer at Delhi do for him and the others?"

So Susan didn't believe in the rosy hope that Governor Wright would grant the petitions!

"If you find a way to read law and pass the bar you would know how to get him freed," she persisted. "Suppose it takes you three years? What's three years against ten?"

She was leaning forward on her little stool, arms locked around her knees, looking at him intently. "Isn't it what you want to do, anyway?"

He whittled more slowly. "How can I give up this farm? It was to have been Gerrit's."

"You can't stay here ten years," she reminded him. "Yes, Walt, you've got to give it up. Not until after next harvest, perhaps, but by then you must find a place to read law and prepare to save Gerrit yourself, as well as make your own way. I thought if you had the statute book you'd be able to get a little start. Especially since you haven't been able to study with Pastor Camp this winter."

"I appreciate the book, Susan," Walter told her, his voice more gentle. "I didn't expect you to even think of it, and I can find an hour to study each night. I've done it before. Only we can't wait years to help Gerrit. Pastor Camp knows of an honest lawyer. I've met him myself. In the meantime there's this sugar harvest."

"Maybe I can help with that more than you think," Susan said, leaving her little stool for the spinning wheel. "I've talked to all the parents. They know what we're up against and they're going to let me close school during the sap run. Three of the older girls and four boys are going to move right in and help us operate the sugarbush."

"What?" Walter dropped the stick with a clatter and stared at her.

142

"You have to start collecting sap about three in the afternoon," Susan said in a matter-of-fact voice. "With you and four boys collecting, you can bring it all in by five or six o'clock, and the girls and I can have everything ready for boiling. If it takes twelve hours to boil it down and get it into the molds, we'd be done by six in the morning. Lou can have breakfast ready as soon as we get back from the saphouse, and we'll have time enough to sleep and be back in the sugarbush early in the afternoon."

"And they'll let you do that?" Walter could hardly believe it.

"Don't forget that Gerrit's paying the penalty for a crime more than one of them committed," Susan reminded him.

It was true and the farmers of the neighborhood had not forgotten. Susan closed her school and the Harrison home became the scene of a sugaring-off bee like nothing any of them had seen before. Laughter rang in the late winter air from the time the boys and girls woke up for the hearty meal Lucretia had ready, until the eerie hours before daylight when they crawled into the beds she improvised, with blankets and cowhides and deerskins on the floor.

Each evening when Lucretia brought kettles of steaming food to the sugarbush, the boys and girls stopped long enough after eating their supper to enjoy one pan of jackwax. Susan always made it, raising the temperature briefly under a small kettle of syrup until it boiled briskly. Then she would turn it onto the clear snow outside, using a slender stick for twirling it into a layer of delicious wax. All of the time her young helpers would be shouting instructions, chasing each other in the snow around the bonfire they had built, singing, and finally smacking their lips over the sweet, thickened syrup.

"It's good they can be happy," Walter said to Lucretia who had taken Susan's place inside the saphouse to help him keep an eye on the huge kettles that were setting up a gray mist of steam. "Another half hour and they'll all have to be in here stirring and skimming the rest of the night. It gets to be tedious work before morning."

"I don't begrudge them their fun," Lucretia said, "only how can I take part in it so long as . . ."

She didn't finish her sentence. One of the boys appeared in the doorway calling to Walter through the cloud of vapor that separated them.

"There are a couple of men here to see you, Walt."

"A couple of men?" Walter repeated. Who could it be? He propped his skimmer safely in an empty gathering bucket, glanced at Lucretia whose expression of concern deepened, and went to the door.

Standing by the bonfire, talking earnestly to Susan was Peter Ten Nuys. Behind him a mounted rider held the reins of Peter's horse. In the darkness beyond the bonfire Walter could not see his face.

Walter stared in silence. What had brought Peter here? What was he saying to Susan? They were so absorbed that for a time neither one looked in Walter's direction. When they did, it was Susan who spoke first.

"Walter, this is important news," she said motioning Peter toward the entrance where Walter stood.

Peter took a few steps toward the saphouse but stopped when Walter did not respond. They stood for a moment looking at each other and when the silence became uncomfortable Susan spoke again.

"Please tell Walter," she said.

Peter took a long breath. "It's a message from the patroon to all tenant farmers," he began kicking awkwardly at the snow. "The farms in Rensselaerwyck are for sale."

"For sale?" Walter could not conceal his astonishment.

144

He had no welcome for Peter but he did need to know more. "What do you mean?" he asked.

"Just that," Peter said but he was eager to talk. "The patroon will sell any farm for a sum that will yield him the annual rent when the money is put to interest at six percent. He's accepting as little as one-fifth for the first payment."

The offer amazed Walter. He recalled his father telling of an offer made once before, but that was years ago and the price so high that no farmer could take advantage of it. Remembering his father, he confronted Peter.

"Why tell me?" he asked. "Why come here to tell me instead of my father?" He was beginning to wonder if Peter had made this news an excuse to see Susan. Peter knew Walter could not buy the home farm nor any part of it. For all he was glad to hear the news, Peter's appearance here at the Harrison farm was an intrusion that Walter resented.

"I've told your father," he heard Peter saying. "It's been my business to tell all in our jurisdiction. He hasn't taken any steps to buy so we decided you should be notified, as the next in line."

As the next in line! So Peter and his father had written Gerrit off as done for! Walter's resentment mounted and he took an angry step in Peter's direction.

"Nobody knows better than you why my father can't take advantage of that offer, Peter Ten Nuys!" he declared. "Until Gerrit is freed from the cell you sent him to, we have no money for anything but his defense."

"It was my responsibility to tell you. To tell everyone," Peter said defensively. "The tenants are able to borrow at the banks for the down payment when they have good farms like yours. But the offer doesn't hold good forever."

Walter wanted to tell him to go away with his good news. If Pa had not taken steps to buy his farm, it was as Walter thought—because he must save the money to engage a lawyer for Gerrit, should there be no pardon. Walter had nothing to say to Peter and while they stood facing each other once more, the other horseman rode into the circle of light from the bonfire.

"You've done your duty, so let's move on," he said. "Little thanks you got, I'd say."

Walter had never seen the man before but he stared in wide-eyed astonishment at the horses. Two chestnut animals, dark manes and tails flowing in the winter breeze, moved with elegant grace into the firelight. Morgan horses, like the one with the white foot!

Walter raised a hand to stop Peter and his companion. Where had they gotten those horses? But he didn't need to ask the question for he knew the answer. There was only one place where Peter could have secured the mount he rode. Could the white-footed one have come from the stables of the patroon too? If it had, someone high in the ranks of the powerful landowner had risked discovery and disgrace to ride with the Delaware "Indians" on that fatal August day.

Someone with influence? Someone like Horace Greeley who had been able to save two of the Delhi victims from the gallows?

Walter walked back into the saproom scarcely seeing Susan or Lucretia or the boys and girls. He knew what he must do as soon as it was possible. He must go to Albany. There might be a way to save Gerrit and Pa's farm too.

Chapter 13

Spring came early, on the heels of the sap run, in a fury of torrential rain that dissolved the last snows of winter and a gale that tore dead branches from the trees, hurling them through the thickening air with lethal force. The storm caught Walter on his way home, too far from the Harrison farm to turn back. But he didn't want to turn back. He must talk to his father, get to Albany, and return to start the spring work, for the land would be ready as soon as the frost was washed out of it.

He rode cautiously, with Pastor Camp's home in mind. The minister might have news, or if none, at least shelter against this wild day.

The main street of the village was deserted when Walter reached it. Tied to the hitching post in front of the vicarage, tails to the wind and heads low, were two horses that Walter immediately recognized—the horses he had glimpsed in the sugarbush. Someone from the patroon's domain was with Pastor Camp. It could be Peter and his father, preparing at last to make use of the letter of recommendation to Charles Stanton. Walter shivered, pulled his wet coat collar tighter around

147

his neck, and went on. It was only a few more miles and not yet dark. He and the horse could see the ruts and stones and washed out gulleys through the sheets of cold rain.

No one saw him when he rode down the lane to the barn-yard, and Ned's welcoming barks were drowned out by rumbling thunder that echoed and re-echoed through the gray-green hills. Wind-whipped, thoroughly drenched, sneezing and coughing, Walter finally stumbled into the kitchen of his home, once more to astonish Pa and Ma.

"Walter!" They were both on their feet at once, hurrying to him and pulling at the wet coat that clung to his soaked shirt beneath.

"John, go get dry clothes at once," Ma ordered his surprised younger brother. "Get Pa's. Walt's too big for your things. Too big for his own, for that matter."

"What brought you here in this storm?" Pa asked anxiously. "Is anyone sick?"

"No, but I want to talk to you about going to Albany to see Charles Stanton," Walter explained while he changed to dry clothes in front of the fire. "If we knew how much he would charge to take our case for Gerrit, we'd know whether you could manage to buy the farm too."

"I thought of that, so I talked to Pastor Camp and Dr. Butler," Pa said, picking up Walter's soaked boots and moving them away from the direct heat of the fire. "People think we should wait until the next election, then if there aren't pardons, we should try the courts. Only no one trusts the courts," he added. "That's why we're all hoping for pardons."

"But even with time for another crop you didn't take up the patroon's offer to sell," Walter said. "I know, for Peter came to the Harrisons."

"I can't buy, Walt," Pa said avoiding Walter's eyes. "If this has to be a court case it'll take all I've saved and maybe more. It can drag on and on. Whatever it takes, we gave Gerrit our promise and I can't rest easy with my first-born in jail."

"Nor can I. So the sooner we find out whether Stanton will take our case, and the size of his fee, the better," Walter said.

"Well, you can't go to Albany in those clothes," Ma announced picking them up from the chair where Walter had spread them out to dry. "No respectable lawyer would take our case. Besides, I'd be ashamed to have Pastor Camp's relation see you looking like this."

Walter hadn't thought about how he looked, but when Ma mentioned it he knew she was right. His suit was shabby and he had outgrown the sleeves and trouser legs.

"The shoe cobbler should be here any day, and you need new boots," she went on. "Wait over until he comes. I've some lightweight lindsay woolsey ready for spring suits and I'll make you one from that."

It was the first of a series of delays that kept Walter from going to Albany until late May, but he was glad indeed to feel well-dressed when at last the great city came to view. Riding out from the spring-green hills it was suddenly before him, beyond the low pasture land and across the Hudson. Walter caught his breath at the sight. White sails on the magnificent river, white clouds in the blue above, and between them towering hills with rows of buildings crowded together, from dark warehouses crouched at the water's edge to white steeples reaching for the sky.

Walter reined in his horse to sit and stare. How had he dared think he could come to Albany and find Charles Stanton? Above the low buildings at the water front were streets with three-story structures and he counted the spires of eight churches from where he sat. In the center of town, halfway up the hill, was a square building larger than the rest, and the rounded dome told him this was the capitol. Beyond it and above were street after street of houses, and finally the bare hill top crowned by rows of lombardy poplars.

Sleek cattle and sheep grazed contentedly in the lush pasture beside the road where Walter had stopped. Squirrels frisked in the elms and maples and familiar bird calls mingled with the melodious songs of warblers. How comfortable this farm land, how bewildering the city ahead. He had told himself he would find the Van Rensselaer estate and its stables and horses, too. It had all seemed so easy back in the Harrison sugarbush, but now where was he to start looking, either for the lawyer's office or the landowners' estate?

The capitol! John Young, the assemblyman from Livingston would be at the capitol and he would know where to find Charles Stanton.

It wasn't difficult to make his way to the great central building for it was plainly in sight, dominating the city. Walter rode slowly past the wharf where two sailing vessels were discharging passengers and cargo. The place was crowded with two wheel carts, noisy with men shouting and dogs barking. In front of the Shamrock Bar an argument was in progress. Walter hurried past the shops where signs advertized weighers and ship chandlers and up into town where elegant carriages and fine horses replaced the carts and draft animals on the dock. But even here there were squat and knock-kneed blacks and bays like his own, and as many people wearing homespun and short jackets as gentlemen with knee-length belted coats and trousers of light manufactured goods, he observed as he tied his horse at a hitching post.

He didn't know what to expect inside the capitol but certainly not the angry voices that came to him when he mounted the steps. He reached the door just as a man was being pushed out of the building. He stumbled against Walter's sturdy shoulder, regained his footing and forced his way back inside, Walter following.

"Young got his victory by smart parliamentary maneuvering, and don't you dare say anything else!" A red-faced man shouted the words and others joined him.

"I suppose you Whigs and Barnburners want the back-clearing farmers here in the assembly," came the retort of the man who had almost knocked Walter over.

"Their representatives are here now, and more a-coming!"

Excitement vibrated through the halls where groups of men jubilantly congratulated each other or stood glumly and quietly aside. Walter listened, trying to put the bits of conversation together.

"This debate between Horatio Seymour and John Young will go down in history!"

"Young had only 58 votes and Seymour 70 when they started. But what astute leadership!"

"Getting the Crain Bill through was the smartest work this assembly has ever seen!"

"Seymour, with all his polish and eloquence and learning! And the backing of the wealthy! I still can't believe he could be defeated by . . ."

"Careful! Careful what you say."

Walter had no knowledge of what the Crain Bill involved, but John Young was the man Charles Stanton had championed at Berne two years before. He turned from the argumentative group to a man standing apart from the others, watching silently.

"Where is Mr. Young?" Walter asked. "Where can I find him?"

"Right there in the center of that group." The man pointed. "Don't you know him?"

Walter shook his head.

"The one with the dark hair and long nose. Most of the others haven't any hair."

Walter saw a man with deep-set, almost hollow eyes, his mouth a straight line even when he smiled, a few dark whiskers under his chin. He was dressed in tightly fitting light-colored trousers, a dark coat that extended almost to his knees, a high white neck stock and flowing black tie. With everyone congratulating him he appeared cautious, disciplined, and almost as cold as Charles Stanton himself. This was the man the lawyer so admired and Walter could understand why. Courage and daring molded the face and bearing of the man, with no trace of vainglory over the victory he had won, however important it might be.

"That's Ira Harris congratulating him now," Walter's sober companion continued. "You're a farmer aren't you?" he asked looking at Walter's homespun suit and heavy boots. "Well, they're your men!"

He sounded disgusted and started away. Turning to see where he went, Walter almost collided with Charles Stanton.

"Mr. Stanton! I beg your pardon! It's you I came to see."

Charles Stanton drew back in surprise, but in seconds remembered Walter and extended a hand.

"Yes, I remember you. Yes, indeed. Walter Platt." His lips didn't smile but the guarded friendliness, the questioning look were in his eyes again. "You came to see me? Here?"

"I didn't know where to find you but I knew Mr. Young would, so I came here," Walter explained. "I didn't know anything important had happened. I guess this isn't a good day for me to be at the capitol."

"On the contrary, it's a day for you to know about. John Young just forced a bill through that provides for a Constitutional Convention."

It was the nearest to enthusiasm Walter could expect

from Charles Stanton, who was looking toward Young and the dignified, well-dressed men who surrounded him. The lawyer was one of them of course, and wanted to be with them now. Before Walter could ask a question about the meaning of a Constitutional Convention they were calling his name: "Stanton! Great day!"

"When can I see you?" Walter asked.

"Can you come to my office tomorrow?" Mr. Stanton asked. "It's on this next street leading down toward the water front. You'll see the name on the sign. There's a bookstore next to it."

They set the hour at ten o'clock.

Walter watched the lawyer move across the room, one shoulder swaying downward with his uneven gait. The circle around John Young opened to admit him and hands clapped him on the shoulder.

This was where Walter wanted to be! A lawyer, working for honest laws and fair courts. A man respected by his fellow men, because he stood for justice and fought ably and well for the principles he believed in. A statesman like John Young. A lawyer like Charles Stanton.

There had to be a way! He couldn't try to take Peter's opportunity from him even if it were possible, but there had to be a way for Walter to study law. He thought of the statute book Susan had bought and wished he had spent more time with it.

He left the building slowly, wondering about the significance of a Constitutional Convention. Tomorrow he could ask Charles Stanton. Now he had the rest of the day on his hands, and another errand. He must find an inexpensive place to spend the night, a livery stable for his horse, and learn the location of the patroon's stables. He rode down the street Mr. Stanton had pointed out, looking at the stores on either side. Never had he seen so many places of business in his life.

He came to the law office sooner than he expected. It was a small white frame building with a hitching post in front, so Walter tied his horse and prepared to look around. There was a possibility that Peter had started his studies with the law firm at last. Walter had seen nothing of his one-time companion since Peter had come to the Harrison sugarbush and his father only knew that Peter had not been in evidence at the village store or tavern when he was there. Certainly Walter did not want to see Peter here and now, but the front door of the office was open so someone must be there.

Walter walked to the bookstore adjoining, from where he might glimpse the interior, but his eyes were immediately attracted to the display. A badly lettered sign read "Used Books Cheap" and in the center was a large volume of Blackstone's "Commentaries on the Law of England." From the little he had learned, Walter knew the value of Blackstone.

How much was *cheap*? If he rode back across the river to the pasture lands he had passed and found a place where he and the horse might safely spend the night . . . if he bought a loaf of bread instead of paying for a meal . . . His hand went into his pocket and fingered the cherished Sheffield knife with the silver bar in the haft.

"Looking for something in particular?"

The voice startled him. A man with a visor shading his eyes had come to the door of the shop and looked at Walter inquiringly.

"No . . . or that is, yes. I was going to inquire where I'd find the Van Rensselaer estate. The pastures and stables, I mean."

The clerk took in Walter's homespun suit, apparently abandoned the thought of a sale, and gave the directions.

Another look through the law office door revealed nothing but a high oak desk, an empty chair and a door leading to a room beyond. Walter untied his horse and rode away from the business section slowly, thinking of the Blackstone volume and wishing he had dared to inquire the price.

There had been so many rigs in the streets, so much noise and confusion, that Walter was only half-conscious of pounding hooves behind him and voices shouting as he rode down a residential street. The words finally came clearly: "Out of the way, ahead! Out of the way, fool!"

A small boy who had been slowly kicking his way along ahead of Walter looked back and dodged to one side quickly.

"It's a race," he shouted. "They're always racing!"

Walter turned to look behind him. Two horsemen were almost upon him, shouting and lashing at their straining beasts, faces tense, bodies low over the necks of their racing mounts. One was Peter Ten Nuys and the chestnut horse he rode beat the turf with one white foot as he dashed forward, well ahead of the other.

This was the horse!

Walter tried to get his slow animal out of the way of the racers but they were abreast of him too soon. Peter's companion cursed at Walter when he crowded past and struck the bay with the butt of his whip. Frightened, the farm horse jumped to one side, missed its footing, and was down on one knee before Walter knew what had happened. Clutching at the saddle, he wondered by what miracle he had not been thrown into the loose rocks and gravel at the side of the road.

Dismounting to calm him trembling horse, Walter at once saw that the animal had been injured. A sharp rock had broken the skin and cut a jagged wound just below the knee. This would have to be washed and tended right away, before dirt and flies got into the raw sore. Once more he bent over to examine the gash, hoping it was not as bad as he first thought. When he straightened up Peter was beside him, holding his panting horse by its bridle. There was no mistaking the animal now that Walter once more was close to that beautiful waving mane and lordly arched neck.

"I was afraid its leg might be broken," Peter said without any preliminaries. "Jason forgets everything when he's racing. Is it all right?"

Walter had never seen Peter so fashionably dressed, so much one of the gentry. He looked ahead to where Peter's companion had stopped in the road. He, too, was a handsome young man and wearing manufactured clothes like Peter's.

"Does the patroon let you have his horses any time you like?" Walter asked, ignoring Peter's inquiry.

"We'd been on business." A defensive note crept into Peter's voice. "We just decided to race the last mile back."

"Some day the patroon's going to catch you," the boy who had warned Walter shrilled accusingly. "Look what you did!" He pointed to the bleeding leg.

"Take the horse to the blacksmith Ned Jones," Peter said, giving the directions. "He's a good veterinarian. We take our horses there when anything's wrong. Tell him I'll pay the bill."

We, Walter thought to himself, more surely referred to the patroon whose horse Peter was riding, than to Charles Stanton.

"You didn't strike my horse," Walter reminded Peter. "If your friend Jason doesn't offer, I'll pay it myself."

The volume of Blackstone went with those words, but Walter could not accept anything from Peter, and Jason made no move to even come back and see what had happened. Walter turned the horse around and started back slowly, without another word.

The veterinarian proved to be a friend of the farmers rather than the patroon, and an outspoken talkative man.

"Those young daredevils who hang onto the patroon's coattails!" he scoffed when Walter told his story. "Racin' and drinkin' and dancin' with the perty girls! That's all that's in their heads. Because they do Van Rensselaer's errands for him, they get invited to the mansion now and then. It gives 'em somethin' to boast about at the taverns."

He charged only twenty-five cents for washing the wound and putting a salve and bandage on the leg.

"If its appetite gets bad, boil down some tamarack and mix a little with his feed," he advised.

Walter thanked him, his eyes on an open shed adjoining the blacksmith shop where an old wagon and several broken wheels were waiting for repair.

"Walk him around a little tonight, and ag'in in the mornin' so the leg don't git stiff," the veterinarian went on. "Tie him up in the shed here for the night, if you'd like."

Walter felt certain the man knew that he, too, would spend the night in the wagon shed. His horse might not appreciate it, but Peter had done him two unintentional favors today. Walter had identified the chestnut horse for a certainty and now he could save his money.

In the morning Walter stopped in front of the bookstore again before he went to the lawyer's office. The volume of Blackstone was still there and so was the sign. Before he left Albany he would find out the price—perhaps he would even own the book—but now there was a more important item of expense to be discussed, and he was more nervous than he had expected to be when he mounted the two steps and stood on the narrow stoop in front of the lawyer's door. What was the proper thing to do, knock or walk in as though it were a store?

Charles Stanton solved the question by opening the door while Walter hesitated.

"Good morning. You're right on time. I saw you from the window."

"There was no reason for me to keep you waiting," Walter said, his eyes taking in every detail of the reception room with its straight-backed chairs, where they paused briefly. Over the fireplace a large map of the United States had been tacked. Framed certificates hung on the walls, and in one corner a high stool was shoved against an elevated table. A place to read and study Walter thought, for it was between two windows and candles with reflectors had been placed advantageously on a shelf above.

It was the private office beyond that amazed Walter when he saw it. One entire wall was lined with books. Never had he seen so many books. He was still staring when Mr. Stanton motioned him to a large, rush-bottomed chair while he took his own seat behind a massive table with a green felt cover. There were other chairs in the room—four ladder-backs all of a dark red wood Walter had never seen, and on the white marble mantle a carved clock ticked majestically.

Mr. Stanton tilted his chair back against a huge iron safe and looked at Walter for a moment before he spoke. "You had something important on your mind, you said. What is it?"

"It's my brother Gerrit. Maybe you recall him for he was with me at Berne. He's one of those unjustly sentenced at Delhi."

"Yes, I know." The lawyer thumbed a silver paper knife.

"We haven't much faith in these petitions for pardons," Walter went on. "My father and I need to know how much you'd charge to take Gerrit's case. We'll raise the money if we can, but we need to know the amount. Pa's let the patroon's land sale go by so we can pay you."

Charles Stanton bit his lip and tapped his desk with the paper knife. "When a lawyer takes a man's care he needs to know more than where the money's coming from to pay his fee," he said at last. "Gerrit got an unfair sentence. A monstrous injustice was done at Delhi and it has aroused the whole state. But are you prepared to tell me the whole truth, so I can decide whether I can take this case and still hold to my principles?"

He was looking earnestly at Walter with no smile on his lips and his cold blue eyes were searching, penetrating.

"I'll tell you the truth, yes," Walter replied almost defiantly. "So would Gerrit. We were both at Moses Earle's farm to help the Delaware County farmers. So would you have been if Osman Steele's deputies had forced their way into your home first, and abused your wife and sister, stepped on a baby's hands and shoved it aside a with a booted foot!"

He had left his chair without realizing it, and stood gripping the felt-covered table, looking down into the expressionless face before him.

"Go on," he heard the lawyer saying.

So Walter told him everything. His first ride with Gerrit to protest the lease system and the fire that never was intended . . . his fight in the Harrison kitchen to protect Susan and Lucretia . . . the ride with the masked "Indians" to prevent an unfair and illegal sale . . . the chestnut horse . . . the trial and the testimony that convicted Gerrit . . . the months he and Susan had worked from daylight until after dark to save Gerrit's chance for the Harrison farm.

"And today I saw that chestnut horse again," Walter finished almost triumphantly. "It belongs to Stephen Van Rensselaer himself. It . . ." He started to say it had been ridden by Peter, but remembered in time that he still did not know for a certainty what relationship might exist or be planned between Stanton & Stanton and the land agent's son. He had said enough when he named Peter as the one whose testimony sent Gerrit to jail, but that was a matter of record.

"It seemed to me that a person high enough in the

patroon's organization to be trusted with his horses might be able to help—if he was one with influence," he added.

Charles Stanton motioned Walter back to his chair.

"One with influence wouldn't dare come out in the open and try to help, for he'd lose his influence if he did," the lawyer said. "More likely it was a young hothead out for the fun of it, or an old-timer with a grievance. No, that's not where your help will come from. It will come from John Young and the Constitutional Convention. You came to Albany on an historic day, only you didn't know it."

Walter had forgotten about the Constitutional Convention. He started to ask but Charles Stanton was ready to talk now.

"I don't know how greatly the laws can be changed by the Convention, but there will be changes in this vicious lease system in the next few months. In the courts too, if the members of my profession who think as I do, can force it. We want to abolish the appointment to legal office, and make all such positions elective. Can you think what that would mean?"

He was leaning forward, his thin face almost hollow in its intensity.

"A judge elected by the people might not turn against them so cruelly as was done at Delhi," Walter answered. "That judge had been appointed by the landowners!"

Mr. Stanton nodded as though satisfied with the answer.

"Wait just a few months more, Walter," he advised. "I know it's hard, but wait and see what the Constitutional Convention does. More than that . . ." He stopped and opened the top drawer of his desk slowly. "There's a way you can help Gerrit more than through me," he said, taking a paper out and turning it slowly in his hands. "Are you willing to work in the next election in your county? Can you get your father to work in his?"

"We'll do anything. Anything to free Gerrit!"

"Then tell the people that you have seen the first draft of John Young's promise to free the Delhi prisoners—every one of them—if he is elected Governor in November!"

The paper trembled in his hands, and Walter was almost afraid to take it.

"It won't read just like this," he heard Mr. Stanton saying. "We're just beginning to work on it. Young hasn't even announced his candidacy, but his friends have started. We'll see that he runs as the Whig candidate. We can get a letter from Dr. Boughton who's still in jail, endorsing him. He'll free your Big Thunder, too!"

Speechless, Walter read the paper Mr. Stanton had handed him. It was written carefully, with words scratched out and others written in. When John Young announced his plans, they would read something like these sentences that swam before Walter's eyes.

"If John Young isn't elected, there's still the Constitutional Convention," Walter heard the lawyer saying. "There'll be changes in our court system and after those changes, I'd have a better chance."

"Then you'll take our case?" Walter asked.

"If Young doesn't win and pardon all of them, yes."

"And the fee?" Walter persisted.

"Tell your father to buy his farm if the patroon's offer still holds good," Charles Stanton told him. "He can take care of the fee better if he owns his land."

He was standing up, extending his hand. "One way or another, we'll free Gerrit," he promised.

Chapter 14

Walter Platt walked from the lawyer's office with a feeling that the world was new, and vibrant with confidence. These things Charles Stanton had said were true. The wraith of the rich old Amsterdam pearl and diamond merchant who got the first land grant for fur trade with the Indians, would be buried forever when the Constitutional Convention met next month. The patroon system and its control of the courts would end. There must be a new administration in Albany too, and Walter had a part to play in bringing it about. He must get started.

He stood on the steps of the law office and looked up and down the street, wondering how he could have been afraid to cross the river only the day before. This Albany! He would come back to it, but he had work to do now, at home among the valley farmers where the cry of defiance had started.

Walter turned toward the blacksmith shop where he had left his horse, but the bookstore beckoned. The display was still there, and the battered volume of Blackstone. Yesterday he had been afraid to inquire the price, but today he hesitated only a moment before the window, then walked in boldly, blinking while his eyes adjusted to the dimness.

The merchant finished arranging a supply of paper and envelopes and sealing wax at the back of the store before he spoke. "Did you find the Van Rensselaer place?" he asked, scarcely looking up.

"Yes," Walter replied, although he had not actually been there. "Now that my business is done I want to ask the price of that volume of Blackstone."

The man pushed the visor back from his forehead and peered at Walter in surprise.

"You know what it is?" he asked. "Pretty dull reading for a young fellow, I'd say."

"I know what it is," Walter said and followed him to the window. "How much is it?"

The man had the big book in his hands, apparently ready to name the price, when a figure appeared in the doorway. It was an older man, one shoulder bent lower than the other, and he stood looking at the pile of used books paying no attention to either customer or salesman. There was something familiar about him but Walter could not recall ever seeing him before. His presence seemed to confuse the merchant.

"The book isn't really for sale," he said. "I'll have to tell you there are pages missing. I use it . . . to build up the display."

"But the sign says 'Used Books Cheap,'" Walter persisted. "Even if pages are missing, what's left is as Blackstone wrote it."

"What's there is authentic all right," The merchant hesitated. "What will you pay, now that you know the state it's in?"

Walter had less than five dollars and his knife. He would give it all, even the keepsake if he must, to possess that tattered book. With it and the "Statutes" he had a start. If he must come back to Albany and go from one lawyer's office to another without introduction of any kind, what he could learn would be his recommendation. What beginner ever possessed two law books? He must have that Blackstone.

"I haven't much money left," he began taking it all out and spreading it on the counter.

The merchant shook his head. "No, I'd rather not sell."

Walter ignored the remark. "And this." He took the beautiful Sheffield from his pocket. The silver bar picked up a shaft of light from the window and stabbed at Walter like the blade it encased.

The man at the door coughed and took a step on the creaking floor. The merchant fumbled with the book.

"No, I can't take your knife," he muttered. "If you want the volume . . . as it is . . . all right."

Walter put his knife back and waited while the book was being wrapped. When he left the store the gentleman was gone. Again Walter wondered who he was, why he had stood there listening to the transaction, and where he had disappeared to. In some unaccountable way that bent old man had saved the knife Peter had given him so long ago. Where was Peter now? Racing somewhere with Jason? Off on an errand for the patroon? Or might he soon be coming down this very street to report to Stanton & Stanton for his studies?

There was no time to think about it now. He must get started, and go home by a circuitous route.

Berne—there were people there who knew him as Gerrit Platt's brother. They would listen to what he had to say now.

Pa, of course. Sam Yates and Tom. The old anti-rent Unit led by Yellow Jacket. Pastor Camp. The Harrison's neighbors and the Schoharie anti-rent association.

Walter went over in his mind everyone he should see,

164

everyone he might tell. From farm to farm the news would spread, just as the old tin horns had carried the alarm when a sheriff's raid threatened. Because he was Gerrit Platt's brother everyone would believe him when he said John Young would pardon the Delhi prisoners and Dr. Boughton too.

Never had Walter experienced such fevered days as those which followed. From the first of June until October 9, the Constitutional Convention held its sessions in Albany, and the deliberations were recorded in the *Freeholder* each week. In spite of the pressure of work and the need for time to read his precious law books, Walter went to his home town regularly for the mail. Someone from almost every family was at the post office when the stagecoach came in, and people divided as soon as they had their papers, going either to Pastor Camp's big lawn or to the tavern with Derick Ten Nuys. Each week Walter had a chance to see his father, and with satisfaction they observed the crowd on the pastor's lawn increasing in size.

The final report came at last, and Pastor Camp began reading aloud, scarcely waiting for all the farmers to assemble. The paper shook as he read.

"All future leases limited to twelve years . . . Alienation fines illegal . . . Judicial offices to be elective . . ." He paused and waited for the men to grasp the importance of that last decree.

"All lands declared alodial," he went on, his thin features warming to a smile. "If I know what that word means, it's just the opposite of feudal, and we all know what that means."

Walter knew the meaning of *alodial* and was about to speak up when he saw Peter riding into the village. He went directly to the tavern.

"I wonder what message he's bringing from the patroon now," Walter said in an undertone to his father. Others had

165

seen Peter too, and heads were turning. Pastor Camp glanced briefly in the direction of the tavern and went on reading.

"All fines, quarter sales, or other restraints are invalid on any lease after 1846, but existing leases are inviolate."

"That means you and Mr. Harrison and all the rest are still bound by your leases, unless you can buy," Walter said to his father. "It isn't as good as I'd hoped it would be. There still is work to be done in Albany."

Across the lawns that separated tavern and parsonage, Peter and his father were coming, the yellowed elm leaves dancing at their feet. The farmers, leaning against the porch rail or squatted on the grass, waited in silence and Pastor Camp stopped reading.

"Welcome, Derick. And Peter," the pastor said, folding his paper.

"Peter has a message from the patroon," the older Ten Nuys began, clearing his throat and looking uncomfortable. "The offer to sell the farms in Rensselaerwyck that was made a year ago is being renewed. The prices will vary according to the nature of the land."

He shifted his heavy bulk from one foot to the other and looked at Peter who was ready to talk.

"My father will be at the land office each day," Peter announced. "If there is any more news I'll bring it from Albany."

"Will you bring us the election results next month?" Pastor Camp asked. "I was about to invite everyone to a singing school here, and we'll be eager for the news. I hope you'll both want to join us with the singing, however the election ends."

Peter's face flushed. If John Young should win, it would be another defeat for the patroon. Peter would not like to bring that news.

"You'll be coming out from Albany as soon as it's known who won, won't you?" Pastor Camp persisted. "The election is November third. By Wednesday night the vote should be counted and it will be in the *Herald Tribune* Thursday, but we won't get the paper until the next day at the earliest. We could be sure of the results Thursday night if you'll promise to come."

Peter hesitated. "I'll be coming back," he said at last. "Yes, I'll let you know." Then he and his father started toward the barren old land office where once, in lordly fashion, they had collected rents and issued orders to the farmers who watched them go.

Walter was eager now to take the news to Susan and Lucretia and Mr. Harrison. It was dusk when he rode into the yard, and they were all in the back garden. Even while Walter talked, Mr. Harrison and Susan kept pulling the slate-red beets from the earth, shaking off the soil and breaking away the dried tops. But Lucretia could not go on working. She stood beside him anxiously, trembling hands reaching toward him as though for more news than he had to tell.

"The farm is safe for Gerrit," Walter assured her. "There'll be no quarter sale price to raise, and the lease will be no longer than twelve years. The owner may be willing to sell before that time is up. Van Rensselaer is."

"If John Young can be elected!" Her words were almost a prayer. "In another month we'll know. He could even be home by Christmas." She looked beyond them toward the house, then roused herself from her day dream. "I'll go get supper now."

Walter dropped to his knees beside Susan to share her task.

"There'll be a singing school at Pastor Camp's Thursday after election and Peter's promised to come with the results," he told her. "You've worked so hard and been nowhere. Why don't you and Lucretia get new dresses and come with me? The Harrisons can get along one evening alone. If John Young wins, think what a celebration it will be!"

"No new dresses for us until Gerrit's free," Susan told him. "We still don't know what Charles Stanton will charge to take the case if there's no pardon. But Walter, I think I found out something while you were gone today. Have you ever looked through your precious Blackstone? Examined it, I mean, page by page?"

"No, why?"

"I did. Elias climbed up to where he could reach it and when I grabbed it from him I thought I glimpsed writing on one of the pages in the back of the book. It's been scribbled in by a child and in one place he had printed 'I am Charles III.' Has your Charles Stanton a son?"

"I don't know, but if he has . . ."

"The Stantons could have thrown the book away after the youngster mutilated it, and your book dealer recovered it from a pile of trash, to add dignity to his display!" Susan sounded triumphant.

"There was something strange about that sale," Walter admitted, recalling the incident and the bent figure of the man in the store. "Susan! That was the elder Charles Stanton who stood in the door and kept the merchant from overcharging me. I never saw him but he had the same sloping shoulder."

They looked at each other over the garden row, smiling and sure of their deduction.

"Anyway, I'm glad you got the book," Susan said. "I only wish you'd found out what Peter is doing when you were at the lawyer's office. Or asked Pastor Camp."

"I can't pry into Peter's affairs, Susan," Walter protested.

Then, "You haven't told me whether you'll go to the singing school with me. Everyone will be there."

"You won't be ashamed of me, as I am?" She looked at her broken finger nails and scratched hands. "After harvest is over I think milkweed cream will help a lot. And I can brighten up my best wool dress with some velvet ribbon at the neck."

He dropped to his knees on the path of earth between the garden rows and looked at her, a smudge on the curve of her cheek, her curls whipped by the October breeze and bronzed by the sunset.

"Ashamed of you?" He wanted to tell her how proud he was of her. He hadn't realized it until this moment, and now that he knew he had no words.

Chapter **15**

They had sung all the old favorites through once, and Peter hadn't come. His horse was tied in front of the tavern and everyone at Pastor Camp's home knew he was there, but he had not kept his promise, so far.

"Let's sing Mother Lee's 'Gospel Trumpet,'" someone suggested and they all looked at Pastor Camp to see what he would say. The Shakers made singing an important part of their religion and there was rhythm in their hymns. Ma, at the organ, caught Pastor Camp's nod. The bellows responded to the pressure of her foot with a leathery moan, then the full notes rang sweet and clear and the singing began.

"By her sufferings overcome
And taught the way of self-denying . . ."

Walter and Susan had taken part in the singing as lustily as the others but Lucretia still would not allow herself such happiness. Instead, she had gone to the kitchen to help the pastor's quiet wife with the work of laying out supper for this huge gathering. From the parlor Walter could glimpse the table, set with the deep blue Staffordshire china the women so much admire. There were bowls and platters of food, for everyone for miles around had come, each family bringing a contribution, and all expecting to hear the final results of the election. And Peter was in town, but he hadn't come to the parsonage.

Walter drew Susan away from the crowd standing shoulder to shoulder around the organ. She looked very pretty tonight, with the narrow band of red velvet around the neck of her dark dress, a fresh red bow at the back of her head, and her eyes shining while she sang the gospel hymns.

"Susan, I'm going to the tavern and find out why Peter hasn't come," Walter whispered. "I think it's because Young has won and he doesn't want to show his face here. You tell Pastor Camp."

He took his coat from the pile in the parlor bedroom and slipped quietly out into the cold November night. Dead leaves crackled under his feet and the wind stung his eyes while he hurried across the lawns to the tavern door. He stopped for a second to look at the horse tied there. Unquestionably it was one of the chestnuts Peter had been riding. This might not be a pleasant encounter, he reminded himself.

Walter gave the horse's shoulder a friendly pat and started for the tavern steps but just as he did so a woman hurried up to the door. He stepped aside to open it for her.

"Oh, thank you . . . I wonder if you'd mind . . . I've never been in the tavern . . . it's always so full of men . . ."

She was a large woman and in the darkness he couldn't see her face, but her voice was trembling and frightened.

"If there's anything I can do, of course I will," Walter said, drawing the half-opened door closed again.

"It's Mr. Ten Nuys. Tell him his wife's no better and I wish he'd try to find Dr. Butler. I wish he'd come home, too," she added although Walter judged that was not meant to be part of the message. "It's fearsome, alone in that big house with her so weak and pitiable."

Walter was promising when the door opened and the full light from the big hall fell upon the woman. Her head and shoulders were draped with a dark shawl and below it her full skirt whipped in the wind. It was black with a pattern of small flowers and in a flash Walter recalled the bolt of goods in the store the day he learned that Peter had the letter—the material that had made the disguise which flew through the air and whipped him in the face when the Delaware "Indian" discarded it.

"Wait!" Walter said, stepping aside to let the departing guest have the steps. "Who are you?"

"I'm Mrs. Ten Nuys' sister, why?"

"I thought I recognized you . . . or something. Perhaps it's the dress."

"Yes, yes." She seemed anxious to get away. "We often have clothes alike. I guess we look alike. But now will you give him my message?"

Walter's head was whirling as he gave his promise. Derick Ten Nuys! It was hard to believe, but now that he thought of it there had been much less trouble in his own home valley than anywhere else. Only once had the sheriff tried to hold a distress sale and he hadn't come back to Sam Yates' pasture to complete it. The farmers had stayed away on Rent Day and there had been no reprisals.

Slowly he opened the tavern door and went inside. The hall was empty and compared to the music and laughter in Pastor Camp's parlor, the place was dreary and quiet. From the bar came the clatter of mugs, a blue mist of tobacco smoke, and voices muttering. He crossed the hall and stood in the doorway.

They were sitting across from each other at a long

172

wooden table, Derick and Peter Ten Nuys, the father's back to Walter and his head resting in one outspread hand. Why had Walter never thought of those broad shoulders, rounded and bulging at the arm pits, and legs like tree trunks? No wonder the disguise had split at the seams when he forced his bulk into it.

Peter saw Walter first and the mug he held in mid-air clanked back on the table. Mr. Ten Nuys raised his head, turned on the backless bench to see who had come in, and nodded in recognition.

"Well, Peter, what are you going to do now?" Mr. Ten Nuys asked.

"I'm not going to the parsonage and listen to those yokels celebrate!" He lifted the mug to his lips again.

Celebrate! It could mean only one thing. Resentment at Peter's contemptuousness, surprise at fathoming the mystery of the Delaware "Indian" rider, were lost in the significance of that word.

"Then John Young won!" Walter hurried to the table. "You mean Young won?"

"Young and almost every other anti-rent candidate, right down the line!" In the flickering candlelight Peter's face was flushed and surly but Walter was not thinking of Peter or how this defeat of the patroon might affect him.

"Then Gerrit will be freed! As soon as Young takes office!" The weight of the universe was slipping from Walter's shoulders.

"It's the only consolation I find in it," Peter said unexpectedly. "Think what you will, Walt, I never intended my testimony to send Gerrit to jail."

Mr. Ten Nuys moved along the bench and Walter sat down beside him. They had not looked at each other and no word had passed between them, yet a bond of understanding existed.

"I believe you. I guess I always believed that." Then, unconsciously Walter repeated the father's question "Well, Peter, what are you going to do now?"

"Do? What do you mean?"

"We aren't children any more," Walter reminded him. "You can't go on forever running the patroon's errands and racing his horses."

"Perhaps I'll buy the land next to Pa's manor. Together we'd have an estate."

"No," his father contradicted. "You may as well know the manor isn't mine. I couldn't buy it. Every time the patroon made an offer to sell the farms, I've gone to him but the manor wasn't for sale." His voice grew husky with bitterness. "The rose gardens your mother laid out and loved . . . the orchard and vineyard I planted hoping one day to leave them to you . . . no, they're too valuable for the patroon to sell!"

Peter stared at his father, wide-eyed with disbelief. "But twice or three times he's offered to sell!"

"Not the manor," Mr. Ten Nuys repeated. "I'm no better off than the farmers—nor as well as some—for all I've been land agent all these years!"

"Is that why you've kept after me all the time?" Peter demanded. " 'Keep up with your studies!' 'Enroll at Harvard!' 'Go to Stanton & Stanton!' " His voice mimicked his father's ponderous tone. The old man sighed heavily.

"Peter, I think the time has come for you to decide one thing," Walter said when Mr. Ten Nuys did not answer his son. "What are you going to do about that letter Pastor Camp gave you to Stanton & Stanton?"

Peter shrugged. "I don't like their politics or their crowd," he said. "Don't think the powerful landowners are licked by this one election."

It was almost a sneer. In spite of the injustice his own father had experienced, Peter was still attracted by the elegant life he had glimpsed at the Van Rensselaer mansion in Albany. The look on his face, his tone, and above all his lack of sympathy for his father decided Walter.

"Then I'll tell you what I'm going to do!" Walter leaned over the table, tense, and his throat tight. "I'm going to Stanton & Stanton myself. I'll tell them you have the recommendation. That you were Pastor Camp's choice. But they have a right to choose too, and I have something as valuable as the letter. I have a year's study of the law behind me already!"

For a moment Peter was too surprised to reply. When the full meaning of Walter's defiance came to him he pushed his mug aside.

"Well that settles it!" He sounded almost relieved. "Go ahead, and go back to the church now and tell Pastor Camp and his farmers that they've won, too. But Van Rensselaer isn't out of business and his crest is still the most respected in Albany. Why, he can give me a letter and to a more fashionable lawyer! Why not?" He sounded triumphant.

"He can," Mr. Ten Nuys agreed. "If he knows how little given you are to studying, he won't."

"I can study if there's a point to it," Peter replied. "There might be, just to argue a case against you and win, Walt!" The mug thudded against the bare table top.

How like Peter! The race . . . the excitement of combat . . . the need for a challenge. . . .

"Then let's see you do it!" Walter shot the words at Peter and slipped his hand into his pocket. His fingers tightened over the pocket knife with its silver bar. "Or don't you think the patroon will really back you?"

He got up to go, and with a lurch Derick Ten Nuys straddled the bench after him. This was the incentive that might spur Peter, and the two of them—the old land agent and Walter—understood.

"Mr. Ten Nuys, will you come back to Pastor Camp's with me?" Walter asked. "They're waiting there, all of the people from our valley."

"No, I don't need to go," Mr. Ten Nuys answered. "Pastor Camp knows how I feel. Besides, I left a sick wife at home."

Guiltily Walter remembered the message he had forgotten to give Mr. Ten Nuys and repeated it now. It startled both father and son and they left the inn at once, together.

Walter stood on the steps for a second watching them disappear, dark figures in the dark night. Sometime he and Peter might indeed face each other in friendly combat again. He had done what he could.

The November night was growing colder. Walter ran across the lawns and as he neared the parsonage Susan and Pastor Camp came down the steps, hurrying toward him.

"You were gone so long," Susan exclaimed. "We were about to go and see what detained you."

"What is the word?" Pastor Camp asked eagerly. "Peter knew, of course."

"It's victory!" Walter grasped the minister's arm. "Right down the line, Peter said. But I did something you may not approve."

"What? You didn't fight with Peter again?" the minister asked.

"No, but I told him I'm going to present myself to Stanton & Stanton and ask if I can read law with them," Walter said. "Peter'll never use that recommendation you gave him, and for a year I've been studying, all the time I could find. What do you think they'll say? Am I being too bold?"

"They'll say you've been a long time coming," Pastor

176

Camp told him. "They've been expecting you ever since the Berne convention."

"What?" Walter couldn't believe it.

"Gerrit told Charles all about you while you were dealing with Peter that time, but I guess he didn't think to tell you," Pastor Camp explained. "Now let's get back to the parlor. There are anxious people there, waiting for your news, Walter."

"You tell them," Walter urged. "It should come from you."

He took Susan's hand and held her back when the minister went inside.

"What do you think of what I did?" he asked her.

"You did it honorably, and it's what we both wanted you to do," she told him.

"But I'll be away a long time. I won't be seeing you every day, like now."

"You might." She sounded teasing and happy too. "Do you remember the first time I saw you? When you came to the Harrison's with Gerrit?"

"Yes, I remember."

"I was all ready to go to Albany to the Normal School. It had just opened the year before. But the raiding party came and Lucretia was so terrified and Elias so little. They seemed to need me."

"So you took the test and taught the common school instead," Walter finished. How well he recalled the night when she had told him of that decision. He had been proud of her then, and was more so now that he knew what she had given up to do it. "You never told me you had planned to go to the Normal."

His hold on her hand tightened. "We can both be studying then, at the same time, and in Albany!"

"It's what I've been planning in my own mind for a long time," Susan admitted. "Sometimes I didn't think it would ever work out."

"But it has. Everything's worked out." He put his arm around her and together they started up the parsonage steps. He hoped she would keep on planning for them both, and never stop.